12 ⁹⁵

THE ANGEL OF SOLITUDE

THE ANGEL OF SOLITUDE

MARIE-CLAIRE BLAIS

translated
by
Laura Hodes

Talonbooks   Vancouver   1993

Published with the assistance of the Canada Council

Talonbooks
201 - 1019 East Cordova
Vancouver, British Columbia
Canada V6A 1M8

Typeset in Palatino by Pièce de Résistance Ltée., and
printed and bound in Canada by Hignell Printing.

First printing: October 1993

The Angel of Solitude was first published by VLB Éditeur,
Montréal, Québec.

Canadian Cataloguing in Publication Data

Blais, Marie-Claire, 1939-
        [Ange de la solitude. English]
        The angel of solitude

        Translation of: L'ange de la solitude.
        ISBN 0-88922-337-8

        I. Title. II. Title: Ange de la solitude. English.
PS8503.L33A7813 1993   C843'.54   C93-091901-7
PQ3919.2.B6A7813 1993

The Angel of Solitude, or a creature that becomes more and more inhuman, crystalline, from which emanate streams of a music derived from the opposite of harmony, or, rather, a music that is what remains when harmony is used up.

—Jean Genet, *Querelle de Brest*

Part 1

Johnie's World

Johnie was casually smoking her cigarettes, it was night, almost dawn. Johnie, Gérard, Polydor, Doudouline were together again in Abeille's* room and Doudouline was saying in a melodious voice, "Abeille's not back yet on this night of the full moon. You saw her leave, girls, her short little leather jacket hanging just above her butt, her headphones on her ears, her cowboy boots on her feet — all set to hang out in the park, I'll bet. It's four o'clock in the morning and we're stuck here waiting up for her drinking beer. Don't get drunk, Polydor, we'll eventually go back to our place, wherever 'our place' is. We can't live with Thérèse and Abeille forever, girls, doing nothing, in perpetual idleness. Think of my mother. At my age she was already being invited to perform in Paris ..." And Polydor let herself be rocked by Doudouline's sultry voice, for Doudouline was there, draped cozily across Polydor's knees, her rosy opulence at rest, and Polydor contemplated her with love-struck eyes; at last she was there, seated

---

* Translator's note: Abeille's name appears in the original with a demonstrative article — "L'Abeille" — a device that serves to objectify or categorize the character. This translation will call her "Abeille" for reasons of readability and rhythm in English.

in the cool hollow of Polydor's lap, hanging her blond head, and Polydor asked, slipping morsels of chocolate between her lips, "Isn't this nice, here among ourselves?"

Johnie, so named because of her passion for Radclyffe Hall, was looking at Gérard, languid in Abeille's velvet armchair. To think how we once loved each other, she thought, in my beat-up furniture near the bridge. She had those long eyelashes that caressed her face, those cheeks of marble, those curls of her hair, and suddenly that vision of their legs as they rolled lazily over each other in the king-size bed they'd bought on credit, and the thought that had separated them in one instant: the future. The future contained in each of them — and that Johnie, by some mysterious ability, read in the cards — had plunged both of them into a fearful meditation, as if they had measured with their bodies, kissing and touching each other in the most sensitive places, how modest their aspirations in life were. "It's freezing in here," Gérard had sighed, lying without a shiver against Johnie's bony frame and hard flanks as they listened to mushy songs on the radio. Gérard was peaceful, almost as if she were in a swoon, and Johnie had felt beneath her that collection of bones, of skinny ribs, as she thought about that faint difference between them, the hair in curls, the black crown of hair that concealed Gérard's marble cheeks, her curling eyelashes, and those slow, lazy movements of Gérard's when she was falling asleep next to a woman, exuding all around her quiet, enigmatic night. (So it was that those names, thought Johnie, Doudouline, Gérard, Abeille, belonged only to them, to the call back from their private places of refuge, their shelters; once they fled the magical retreat, would they not be as vulnerable and naked as soldiers stripped of their camouflage in a forest where the cunning enemy could be lurking behind every tree?) "I bet she's in someone's arms," said Doudouline to Polydor. "She always loses her head on the night of the full moon." Abeille must be wandering in the streets, in the parks, her agile and shivering Abeille. It would occur to her to go walking shamelessly at night, in search of a suspicious creature who would coax her — wasn't it scandalous — and yet you couldn't scold her for it, it was the time of her period, the madness of the blood that ate at her. Sinister things our insides are, Doudouline thought, and Mother, for all that, my poor mother, to go to so much effort to give birth to me, ready to deliver on-stage as she played Racine, and I do nothing with my hands, I write a bit of music, I have an amazing voice, say my instructors, but what good is it to attack your work so furiously when you're young? Save that for old age, as Gérard would say. Fine, so Abeille is still with a man, some hoodlum, no doubt, that she bumped into — all those people who lie in wait, gathering their strength in a shady park at that hour — her feet sweating in her boots, her ears ringing with rock music. And it was true that for Abeille that shattering music seemed to pour forth from the vault of the sky, from the bare-branched trees, from the earth that shivered beneath the frost. As soon as a man opened the door of his car to her she got in next to him, passively let herself be taken in his arms, it couldn't be otherwise, thought Abeille, a fatalist, for the moon was red and high in the sky, but she had forgotten to feed the cat before she went out, and the painting — the painting was still unfinished in the living room. "You will be *the* painter of our generation," Doudouline had told her, and now in the smoky living room everyone was turning towards the painting that Abeille had done; it was a portrait of Thérèse, *Thérèse* or *The Pleasures of Summer*. In it Thérèse was stretched out on the grass in a striped bathing suit; nailed to the middle of the wall, the painting, like the girls contemplating it, seemed to be resting in a pensive lethargy. Gérard had gotten up from her chair with her usual languor saying that it was time to go to the bars before they closed, one had to warm oneself somewhere this dismal, endless winter, she sighed in Johnie's ear. Then she had gulped down her Coke while Johnie was writing in her notebook — what a drag to be preparing for a degree in German, to be on a scholarship at the university like Johnie, with her parents — engineers who had raised her among piles of old papers and books — and one might have believed sometimes that Johnie was a victim of that passion for the written word, the divinely possessed fervor that made Gérard so jealous. A shame to miss out on the true life that ran in the bars in that thin thread of light at dawn, thought Gérard, and Johnie raised her head from her notebook towards Gérard who was ready to go out, dressed in her red dinner jacket, you could see the ears of her Mickey Mouse T-shirt poking out from beneath the silk of her blazer. Johnie closed her eyes, letting the smoke from her brown cigarettes veil her face. "And who do you hope to meet at this hour?" Doudouline asked Gérard with severity; she was bent cozily backward over Polydor's knees and the authority in her voice was startling in the vaporous disorder that was expanding everywhere with the beers and cigarettes in Abeille's living room. And downstairs Abeille was slipping on her clothes, even the heaviest ones — the fur hat and the mittens — and, suddenly thrown out into the freezing night, she was meditating under the sky on her morosity, her dangers. He, the man, put his hand on Abeille's shoulder, he shared his melancholy thoughts, saying he was nothing but a humble taxi-driver and it had been good of Abeille to make love with him. "Disappeared after five years of living together," Abeille was saying in a low voice, her eyes shining coldly behind her glasses. Yes, but hadn't Doudouline incessantly repeated "You're going to lose Thérèse, you never finish anything, neither paintings nor drawing courses, you go out at night, you're going to lose Thérèse," and with Doudouline's chanting voice that had so often called Abeille back to the order of the clan other sounds were associated, other eloquent murmurs when the girls of the group assembled, day and night, in Abeille's house. There was the indolent Johnie, a swan in the dust of the early morning, sipping her coffee at dawn, and Gérard in her frost-covered backyard from which she poked out only her cheeks, rosy from the cold, hard as apples, she would only offer them forth at an angle, barely displacing herself from the pillar of her rigid torso as if the rain, the snow, had wrapped her delicate jacket around her, rooted there in the foyer, but Thérèse who had left would be no more than a passing loved one in a painting, they would no longer hear her living and breathing, thought Abeille, except in that fateful portrait hanging above the table where Doudouline and Polydor licked their fingers as they buttered their toast in the morning.

The painting glowed with innocence above Doudouline's head, its light suffusing the smoke-filled room with a warm brilliance, and in that light — for the paralyzing light of dawn was also unfurling its way into the room through the windows, the light of crime, thought Johnie, in which you could see everything, even those icicles, that snow piled up on the window-panes, and farther away the neighbors' clothesline and those repulsive socks or briefs that trembled in the wind, materializing foully between the gloomy sky and a jumble of alleyways, filthy houses — Doudouline was dipping her fingers into the jar of jam when suddenly she saw herself again with Polydor and her mother in Paris: They were going into Sophie's dressing room, crushing their slender idol under bouquets of roses: "We have no money for the ticket back, Mother dear ... we needed new clothes, we weren't going to come see you act in Paris in our dirty jeans." And Sophie, who was more than a mother, a goddess rather, or at least a princess of her art, thought Doudouline, looking out the bleak window where the neighbors' clothesline was bouncing in the wind, had pushed the girls aside crying "Why did you give me children, oh God — they all think I'm a millionaire!" Yesterday's papers had said that Sophie had been startling in that Strindberg play, and Doudouline and Polydor were going to fling their arms around her entreatingly, but, as actors were invading her dressing-room, Sophie gently, playfully pushed her daughter away — Polydor too, but that couldn't have hurt her as much, thought Doudouline — with feigned detachment, saying "We'll see each other later, my dear," and Doudouline had thought with bitterness, since she's been here, Mother's had an imperiously French accent. And as if she had felt that familiar severe look weighing upon her, Sophie had hesitated slightly. That used to happen between the two of them, that imperceptible slippage of the soul, that habit of wavering under the pressure of a look that was a bit hard, and little by little the range of firm, guarded words abandoned her, and Sophie had said in her most natural tone, "No matter how much we love you, you ravage our hearts," as they heard the cascade of a serious, dispossessed laugh from her pretty mouth, its grace often contracted, for, moved at seeing her daughter again after those long months of separation, she warmed herself in those bonds of sudden intimacy that Doudouline knew so well: "And your brother — is he still a bartender in the Antilles? Is he still snorting coke? What crime did I commit against the good Lord to deserve children like these?" And at the restaurant, among the actors who were toasting her health with champagne, hadn't Sophie suddenly betrayed, in her triumphant drunkenness, those secret miseries — "Yes, my Doudouline, a pitiful salary, the cold attic room, even pneumonia. I couldn't tell you all this in my letters, that's how it is, daughter of mine, when you begin life anew at fifty, but I regret nothing" — while Doudouline looked at her mother with a delicious despondency, forgetting Polydor who was at her side and scolding her as usual for her gargantuan appetites for cakes and cream. "She eats too much, she's always hungry," Polydor was saying to Sophie, and Sophie had laughed an uncomfortable, almost suffering laugh. The complicity of these statements, these indiscreet cooings around the table, had suddenly made Doudouline go pale, imprisoned in her pink flesh, deposited in the abundance of her silk dress — like in a casket, she thought. She would have liked to disappear into the dullness of the day, no longer feel anything, for on the other side of the restaurant window confused, dirty, dying men lay sleeping on the sidewalks of Paris. And what was Doudouline doing? She was moving rich food around on her plate, conscious of her captivity in a voluptuously satiated body, conscious also of the mocking, conciliatory laugh of her mother, who in one instant had filled her with shame.

§

It was seven o'clock in the morning when Abeille came home, her headphones on her ears, the way Doudouline had seen her go out with such restlessness into the night. "Another taxi driver?" Doudouline inquired with a nasty look, but Abeille didn't hear, the music of Michael Jackson was gripping her temples, uniting itself with her cardiac rhythm, as if, in the intensity of those crescendos that ran through her, the blood that she lost each month, which always reminded her of the death of her mother, had begun to hum in her ears, making her fearful of some incoherent recklessness — jumping from a seventh story window, feeling desire for a stranger, seeking the burning contact of a man against her thighs that were blue with the cold — and it was not until the music of "Thriller" had stopped that Abeille remembered where she was, among the girls, in her own dear living room, the corner that served as her little studio, her kitchen that she took such vigilant care of, and everywhere she saw nothing but the clumps of wilted girls, their open beer cans, their cigarettes resting on the edges of chairs, and on the wall, above Doudouline who was eating a slice of pizza, the painting, implacable and proud as ever, flooding Abeille with the consoling presence of Thérèse, who, without separating herself from the work of the painter, had majestically fled as if she were going to the mountain to do her morning jogging, thought Abeille, suddenly mortified, irritated when Johnie stretched herself stiffly at her side and suggested she go to bed, for who was still up at eight in the morning?

Abeille listened to the breathing of the hushed, sleeping house, it was the time that Johnie began writing, opening her notebooks on the table, fixing a sleepy eye on the ends of her pencils. Abeille was removing her clothes, her soaking wet boots, carrying with her from the living room into her little cubicle of a bedroom — for wasn't she the only one with a sense of territory? — one or two cold cans of beer and that all too palpable souvenir of Thérèse and her long Grecian nose, the canvas that still smelled of paint in the living room, that settled down with Abeille at the foot of the bed where from then on only the cat would take refuge, the same submissive cat of the picture that had consented, though not without its caprices, to be painted, to sit still, its forefeet, with their claws that scratched at the folds of the plaid comforter against Abeille's chest at night. How many nights, her head on the pillow, on the most detestable mornings when the sky itself wouldn't come to your rescue, to rain or snow as it did in other places, when all was stagnation under the March clouds, immobile as the ceiling of the bedroom — whose every crack Abeille had counted, each one concealing a secret, a scar that time had inscribed in the plaster, the wood, and so it was with every neglected object in the universe, the multiplicity of cracks finally vanquished you, having become the symbol of the repetition of our acts to the point of exhaustion, the sterility of ennui, a symbol also of our abandonment on the earth, you went to sleep, thought Abeille, tired of understanding nothing about the meaning of life — how many hours of intertwining under the plaid comforter, hours that were chilly even when she was buried in Thérèse's bosom, had Abeille bared her soul in vain to that sensible ear (How sensible, unyielding, Jansenist she was! Didn't Thérèse

17

suddenly have every fault in the world?) that had expressed disapproval when Abeille appeared aroused by alcohol and women, just what was she talking about, what was that negative philosophy of existence, of a sublime letting-go of consciousness that Abeille talked about, pupils on fire, and why were Abeille's pupils suddenly so large, so luminous? Was she tripping, like so many others did? No, Thérèse did not like that slack, easy awareness of living bound to a state of pleasure, of celebration, of dissolution, though the beauty of the present instant was perhaps glorified by it, as time, centering on the self, flew by inversely to the dramas of the world. Rather than building a house with her own hands, helping delinquents or the homeless, learning to use a camera or computer like Thérèse, Abeille was misled everywhere by her sensations of a particular well-being, brief as its pleasures were, be it filtered into the foam of your beer or dispensed by a taxi driver, this savage and headstrong joy was not happiness, Thérèse said, and often Abeille felt those pangs of ennui, as tenacious as the thought of the many cracks in the ceiling, in all the ceilings in the city that hid the sky, the light, the sun. Gérard was taking off her dinner jacket in the kitchen in the midst of a long yawn: the aching of this gesture, its languor, in a kitchen where it was cold, grated on Abeille's nerves as she got up again to get herself another beer. What was the point of a commune of girls — that term had already fallen out of fashion anyway — if each one gave in to her private impulses? thought Abeille looking at Johnie leaning over her notebooks, pushing away the jar of jam and the drops of liquid that clung to the red tablecloth, and why was she writing that essay "From Sappho to Radclyffe Hall"? Weren't there enough women that you could have talked about right here? The universities, the bars were teeming with them and Johnie would soon be rummaging through the European libraries, breathing in the perfume of her dead heroines, thought Abeille. Doudouline, who was hot in any season, was dozing on the mattress near the refrigerator with Polydor whom she held crushed against her, of whom nothing could be seen beneath the thin blanket that cloaked them but the tuft of hair on top of her head. It was strange to think that beneath that disorderly shock of brown hair slept a would-be preacher, a theology student who did not believe in God but wanted to change the social order — as if that were not the goal of each one in this house — when on all sides was rising — and, who could know, more than ever before, the eternal fortress of a comfortable patriarchy that everyone had gotten used to. Abeille would have liked to throw herself into unending discussions on the vileness of religions, though her tongue was pasty with drunkenness, but it was on just such a black and sinister morning that Johnie had decided to begin her work, or the essay on one of those celebrated works of which she spoke so often, that seemed to leave her suddenly suspended in a different world, a world of unrecognizable beauty, thought Abeille, for down here nothing changed; the neighbors' clothesline still squeaked in the wind. Through all the general passivity in the living room, where thoughts centered on laughing or having fun, you would see Johnie, our Johnie, writing, you would hear her thinking profoundly, and Gérard, already on her feet, hung around her and the incomprehensible symbols of her writing, resenting Johnie's fervor — her English mother had to be the cause of it — for books, for writing. Gérard was tapping a foot on the varnished wood floor saying "Hey Johnie! The bars will be closed soon," until her stomping evoked for Johnie the muffled sound of the snow, after the music in the Club, underneath the soles of their shoes as they walked together up the silent streets at dawn. Nervous shivers ran up and down Johnie's back as she bent over the scattered sheets of her notebooks, guilty of subtle treasons when she dared to take up a pencil or pen before Gérard's eyes, she was thinking about Thérèse scaling the mountain with her ample, enthusiastic bounds at six o'clock every morning and wondered what she was doing here awaiting the revelations of the mind in a cold room where you had to blow on your fingers to warm them. "Shh," said Gérard, pulling on the feather baubles that hung from Johnie's ears, "keep working, I won't bother you." Gérard wandered into the kitchen dressed in her Mickey Mouse T-shirt, she came back and let the cat out, noisily slammed the door. "From Sappho to Radclyffe Hall," Johnie was writing, and suddenly, like Thérèse, she found herself again at the summit of the mountain, breathing the thin air of the peaks, and she would have loved to know how to describe, in one honest or lucid sentence, her feeling, which seemed to become increasingly cloudy with her nighttime fatigue. But wasn't this sort of how things were: Society was like a monotonous forest where wildflowers rarely grew, and as if the country were at war and there were soldiers lurking in the grass, camouflaged in that green, monotonous foliage to better lose themselves in the forest; you could no longer distinguish the soldiers from the cunning enemy that hid behind the trees, those trees that had taken on the tint of the forest themselves, everywhere in that monotonous-looking forest. Anyone wearing a different color could trigger the attack of the enemy. But Johnie would soon close her notebooks, for Gérard was divesting herself of

20

her weapons of seduction, piece by piece: the red jacket, the jeans that clung with a studied refinement and revealed the crease of her labia, the red plastic shoes that Gérard's long, slender feet often dragged over the skating rink of the streets and sidewalks, in the mud as well as the snow: "Come at once," cried Gérard "or else I won't be able to sleep, you know me. Where are my pills?" Johnie came to stretch out next to Gérard: she took her time going to sleep in the bushy pillow of Gérard's curls, for the light of day, a shivering, frozen light, was penetrating the half-open blinds and that same thought returned continuously while Johnie listened to Gérard's breathing in her ear — and why was her breathing so rapid, why was it suddenly accelerating? Yes, on the surface all was peaceful, but any man or any woman wearing a different color could at any instant trigger the rage, the hatred of the enemy.

§

Another one of those frigid mornings, thought Abeille, a distressing winter day when you opened your eyes in a bed warm with pleasure that wasn't your own, for so it had been since Thérèse's departure, Abeille thumbing her nose at chastity beneath the plaid comforter. Often she didn't know the woman she was following as she left the dance floor, following her closely, receptive to the animal caress — she would have preferred to keep her headphones on in bed, keep listening to "Beat It," but Paula didn't like Michael Jackson, she didn't like anyone, not Stevie Wonder or Ray Charles either: "Who are all these barbarians?" she'd ask tartly. She sensed like an absurdity the gulf that separated one generation from another, for even between the sheets, alone with Paula, bathing in an intimacy that was foreign to her, Abeille thought, no doubt because Paula had once been her drawing instructor — those courses she'd never finished — and a friend of her mother's, which widened the gap. Be it Michael Jackson or Stevie Wonder, there was no question: Paula was a limited creature. "Are you alright?" asked Paula, "Did you have trouble sleeping? I rescued you just in time last night — one minute more and you would have left with a missionary who had completed her sexual apprenticeship in the bush. You were stepping on her feet while you danced. Even your mother, who was such a liberated woman, wouldn't have approved." Then Abeille had seen the long woman seated in the middle of a dusty ray of sunlight that fell upon the cold floor. There she was like a tall flower in her nightshirt, a sort of surplice, thought Abeille who was holding her head in her hands, heavy as lead. Paula was well-known in the theater world for the originality of her sets and the opulence of her Wagnerian operas. She is an opulent woman, a compelling woman, a tragic woman, thought Abeille, her eardrums deafened, but Paula was also a painter and etcher of extreme sobriety. She was getting out her paintings and etchings now, from a chest that had long been locked. "I'm showing you all this with your mother in mind," said Paula, and Abeille leaned towards Paula's admirable creations spread out on the floor. She admired the purity of the strokes, those lines when Paula sketched a tree, often a tree with no leaves, in a yard with no garden, with no flowers, a tree that stood black and petrified in a far-off and funereal season where Paula had handed over her soul. "How I love your etchings," said Abeille — suddenly

22

reassured, for hadn't the Michael Jackson gulf been bridged now — but Paula had already snatched her portfolio from Abeille's hands saying "No — I was wrong — you cannot understand" and with the doubt that shook Paula to her deepest foundations Abeille felt a powerful, imperious wind pass over her. Paula seemed to emit lightning bolts, even when she was full of doubt, as she was at this moment, the debris left from her time with Thérèse; she banished ennui and chastity beneath the plaid comforter with or without Thérèse, and if Abeille were saved from boredom and even from the dazzling, dangerous, fatal nostalgia that season, she would stop counting the cracks in the ceiling of her bedroom, she could be a painter, an etcher, and Johnie, who had written in her journal what a hostile, unsightly season winter was, thought about those wretched people who went coughing, trembling with fever to the factory, to the office. These same women, these same men begged of the tarot cards that Johnie read for them — but soon she would no longer have time for it with her essay — the verdict held by their destinies.

And Johnie scattered her gold dust over them, lavishing the limitless manna of her experience (which often seemed to have preceded her) somewhere other than her writing. What a general listlessness most people lived in, what banal discipline weighed down their days in those offices, those factories, while all the time, born in a milieu fostered by intelligence and money — and to radically feminist parents — Johnie enjoyed a liberty she might have described as flighty, for Johnie remembered the warmth of Gérard — but why that rapid breathing? — the perfume of her hair that she had buried her face in to sleep. She thought about the fact that while the other girls of the group had only one roof, Abeille's house, Johnie had several, from her parents' house, where she was always welcomed with hasty joy among their numerous projects, the lectures they were preparing, to her own place — the girls knew nothing about what Johnie called "her place" — that secret apartment she shared with Lynda, the door she opened after leaving Gérard's bed. And suddenly she had seen the object: the betraying object, a razor, a vulgar apparatus that a man had left behind that took up all the space in the bedroom. Yes, a man had been there, slept in that very room; Lynda and the man had made love in that bed. Inebriating odors were still wafting from the invaded bedroom; how could Johnie have confided to Gérard, Doudouline, Polydor, let alone Abeille, who became authoritarian so often, that for years she had held a woman hostage? How could she have explained to all of them that she had kidnapped Lynda from the store where she was selling jewelry for her mother? Not familiar with the world of the working class, Johnie had been attracted to it, or what's more, she had to admit, the world that brought out the proprietor's instinct in her. Lynda, however, had never felt the weight of Johnie's tyranny, if she could define the autocracy she exerted over Lynda as such; she demanded fidelity, obedience, but without ever uttering these commandments out loud. But that time Lynda had been seriously disobedient: She had brought a man, not even a student, to the house, and the razor forgotten on the bedside table was the impudent symbol of that masculine invasion; a man had shaved there, in that room, with icy narcissism, splashed his face with aftershave. Lynda had pressed her cheek against that supple cheek, still rough in some places,

24

beneath the stubble, and Lynda had been penetrated by that virile body that rejoiced in its victory till the cry of orgasm. Ah! These unfortunate wives whose fate she studied in the tarot cards, helpless in the face of adultery, a violent crime of the senses that destroyed them — how she pitied them as she stood at the window, her cigarette burning itself out in her fingers. And suddenly Johnie caught sight of Lynda — yes it *was* Lynda getting out of a man's car, confident, radiant in a fur coat — Lynda who was poor, who had for so long represented for Johnie the working class and its struggles and infected Johnie with the desire to love her, or to dominate her with love, how could she have known, now throwing herself into Johnie's arms, rosy with contentment. It was Lynda, and you had to respect the social class she had sprung from; Johnie could shake her a bit, but not severely, with an air of plaintive harshness, never castigating. Johnie remembered the unease she had felt waking up next to Gérard that morning, wasn't it with Gérard that she had given up reflection and discipline, burying herself in Gérard's hair with abandon at night — all because of the dope, that South American hash that Gérard bought cheap in the city bars — that hash cut with tobacco that colored the monotonous days in the grey of winter with its rosy effervescence so that Johnie would sit immobile in Abeille's living room, watching Gérard dreamily take off her plastic slippers that were the latest trend, or fixing her attention on a lone geranium hibernating in a pot. Then there was the episode of Gérard's cap: Strangely, even if our evil deeds repeat themselves, the nail that runs us through becomes sharper and sharper, so these minuscule acts of cruelty are inscribed in that huge book that no one will ever read, for Johnie always said, as she went out for the night with

Gérard, "I'll write that tomorrow." The cap was there, as supreme in its presence as the razor on the bedside table, and these objects contained many pages, like a book that dripped blood. At the same time, there were pages barely worthy of being written, but for Johnie alone her memory preserved those works of art that, for our discomfort, being of no use to anyone anymore, present themselves to us with hostile mediocrity, reminding us of how imperfect we are, each one of these scenes from life representing an often unspoken shame, a deception, like the memory of the razor or the cap. It had happened at the Club: Gérard had snatched a tweed cap away from an anonymous girl she had kissed, leaning towards her slowly, lazily, and that light, grazing caress — and above all that object, the cap that had shielded the kiss, Gérard's mouth and the rosy fruit of her tongue offered to another woman — still tore at Johnie's soul. For beneath the shade of the cap was the offering of an illicit concupiscence that Johnie had not been invited to share. They had exchanged a kiss, an embrace, and Johnie had thought that she would never again sleep next to Gérard, with her uncomfortably hard flanks and her prominent cheekbones. You got hurt around Gérard. Doudouline and Abeille were laughing on the dance floor, and Gérard had just debased herself with that greedy, self-indulgent kiss. And now, all of that same secret humiliation of the instant that inspired Gérard's kiss, just an ordinary instant, brought a lump to Johnie's throat when she saw Lynda again, getting out of a man's car, Lynda with her outlined lips, as delicate as Gérard's, Lynda running up the stairs toward Johnie ready to lie to her. Johnie saw in Lynda's trembling smile that carried the threat of tears that she would tell everything, she was already telling everything in Johnie's arms. Johnie did not push her away but held her head high with dignity; she would have to look at the cracks in the ceiling and practice Abeille's often desperate metaphysical calculations and silently deplore the ennui you could feel living on this earth, with the repetition of our troubles, but what worried Johnie was not so much the misery of ennui as that divine cruelty that eluded the clairvoyance of men. "Johnie, you've got to understand, it'll just be a fling, he's rich, an Arab prince ... Listen to me, Johnie ...." Johnie listened to Lynda's sobbing against her flat, unformed breasts, and, without hesitation, uttered those perverse words: " You've noticed that I often go out at night?" "Yes, with your brother Gérard." "Except, you see, Gérard is a woman," and Lynda, whose thoughts often seemed distracted and confused, wept huge tears. Johnie looked at the grey ash of her cigarette that was shedding itself onto the living room rug, it was a white bear, one of those vulgar objects that Lynda had chosen; like the cap and the razor, the rug was classified among those symbols of misfortune, along with Lynda's low-cut dress and fur coat. Lynda was still crying as she packed her suitcase, and Johnie would have liked to approach her, but she had the impression that she was wasting away among those objects that had defeated her, the prince's razor, Gérard's cap, the luxurious clothing Lynda was packing into her suitcase; Johnie was about to die right there, standing at the window, while the sky was swelling with clouds that were already announcing nothing but cold and snow.

§

And lying listless in her filmy nightgown, Doudouline moved her feet in the filtered light of the lamp, those feet that haunted Polydor, for, charming as they were, like the rest of Doudouline, those feet, the feet of a gay woman, were unknowingly submitted to an ecclesiastic censure that cut them off from the communion of the faithful they belonged to by birth, and Doudouline, reading under the lamp before taking refuge in sleep, was hardly preoccupied with this excommunication, this punishment; she had barely gone to sleep when her dreams transported her to realms of paradise; prairies, gardens full of dazzling colors, where she heard the music of Gounod, grandiose landscapes she spoke of with ecstasy upon waking, as if the rejection from the Church hadn't even touched her, thought Polydor, while Doudouline's rosy flesh, undulating beneath the sheets, was burdened with the most solemn of condemnations. Doudouline, Abeille, all of them forgot, thought Polydor, below the somber line of her eyebrows, that age-old censure that mutilated them each day, in the emancipation, the nascent liberty of their bodies, those bodies that already were no longer theirs, even as they exchanged them inseparably with one another as they were doing now — thus assuring themselves that they were living, interdependent parts of one whole that would always be split apart by the invader — for each one of their organs was before all else the property of a Roman papacy that probed its gynecological lamp into their uterine canals. Abeille would have to be warned that she was always accompanied by those bothersome witnesses, even when she thought she was alone in the park: Saint Thomas Aquinas, the Fathers of the Church, the Inquisition and its judges — bishops, cardinals in their robes scarlet with blood that had been spilled — all of them watched over her sexual urges, everywhere, even in Paula's arms, surrounded by the bed's sensual, arousing aromas and the strong odor of the cigarettes that Paula smoked day and night; everywhere the liberty of Abeille and those like her was compromised, sacrificed. But, laughing and chatting, the girls knew nothing about this; when it occurred to them to go out, it was not to go read the theologians in the library, thought Polydor, but to stamp their feet in the currents that ran with the debris of winter, sniffing at the first stirrings of spring that would soon bring the flowers to bloom. Or to hang out till dawn in Abeille's smoke-filled living room, where, in the hours of evanescence, Gérard fell asleep sprawled over a chair wearing her red dinner jacket. Each one gave off, thought Polydor, the essence of greedy but peaceable flesh, standing or seated, these girls were too refined for the conquest of love, only Abeille took on that consequence-laden labor, with Paula: when she did come home, it was to assure the others that she would start etching with Paula soon, quickly swallowing her bowl of oatmeal on the corner of the table with its red tablecloth, averting her gaze from the portrait of Thérèse above Doudouline, who was buttering her bread. "So you go out, you have fun, you forget your friends," Doudouline was saying. The halo of Doudouline's hair, in the morning light — the thought also that the commune could continue without her — aggravated Abeille's pain, she sought her deliverance elsewhere, be it with a taxi driver or with

Paula and her tubes of color; eager to help all people, Paula gathered from the street, among her numerous female visitors, the starving painters she taught in the evenings, like the sick woman she invited to rest in the kitchen, supplementing her own therapeutic gifts with the perspicacity of her old servant, Madame Boudreau, who had seen Paula at her birth, and described her as, "a little girl who sucked her thumb in an abnormal way, who for a long time was skinny as a spider and so ugly it was frightening, who took a cushion to school because she had boils all over her bottom, her father was so busy with all his patients, there were even some that died in his office in the winter, no time to go back home, they had no breath left in them, medicine was not what it is today, the poor saint of a man would try to make her eat by building castles with the potatoes on her plate." Abeille lived her life divided between the nursing that Paula provided her, the unbending logic of a woman who had had sores on her bottom, who went to school each morning with a cushion, who at five was already wearing wire-rimmed glasses on her beaky little nose, an was telling Abeille today that she didn't know how to "paint a watercolor without making splotches everywhere," and Paula's friends, all her friends, Paula's giving humility that resisted no one and that to her own horror, rejected Abeille, as if she were alone in the depths of her bedroom, surrounded once again by all the cracks in the ceiling. One friend came to do her laundry in the basement, another knocked at the door, holding her poster for Art Nouveau in her hand; "What Art Nouveau?" demanded Paula, but as a precaution she always locked the glass door of the living room behind her, the living room, with its ancient furniture, often covered with a plastic sheet, that had once been her father's doctor's office. There was also that young artist who needed Paula's approval for her clown pageant, and that other one, a distinguished lady to whom Paula had offered a whiskey in an elegant bar that only she frequented, often a married woman whose time of availability was short, between four and six in the afternoon, Paula inflicted fresh bite-marks on her lips and her pearl-adorned neck. Love for Paula was one of life's ordinary activities, like eating or drinking wine, thought Abeille. She came out of her mysterious doctor's office tugging at the zipper of her pants, a cigarette hanging from her mouth, below the wayward mass of her hair, quickly she painted a scene evoking classical Greece for her stage set for the next day, opening a third bottle of white wine that she drank standing up as she painted, sometimes keeping one hand free to draw Abeille nearer, onto her lap, so that Abeille, level with Paula's breasts, could see the dilation of her nostrils, like the swelling throat of a cooing, trembling, sensual pigeon. Paula's nostrils breathed in the aroma of a roast in the kitchen oven the way they coveted a woman; so much gluttony was pleasing to Abeille, who all the same felt a vague uneasiness when her turn came to be coveted, breathed in, and chewed up by Paula: In Paula's greed a shadow of vice was linked to the wire-rimmed glasses on her beaky little nose, to the little girl of five who sank her miserable pointed buttocks into a cushion at school, in silence and an immoderate wisdom. Today Paula was avenging herself: She was hungry, thought Abeille, but still imperturbable in her creative energies, in just a few minutes, she had painted with her vigorous brush strokes, two panels of a Mediterranean sea, and Abeille had had the sensation of being engulfed in them, since Paula's fingers that had kneaded together the blue and ochre, painted the blue sky, the sparkling waves, had also massaged Abeille's shoulders and the nape of her neck, warmed her to the core, but oddly, Abeille had felt sequestered, deprived bit by bit of the fluid air emanating from Paula's painting: She had seen the little girl with the beaky nose, heard the precocious voice that, according to Madame Boudreau, who knew all there was to know on the subject of Paula, had uttered the word "dog" — "And she was right on the mark, a huge Saint Bernard was walking down the street with its master. Did you ever hear of such a thing, a child that spoke before learning to walk ?" — at an age when most kept silent, and Abeille thought how unworthy she was of Paula and the immensity of her strength that crushed her, physically and morally, for Paula was not only the ogre that satisfied her appetites day and night but also the creator of the charred black tree, portrait of an invisible distress that Paula had etched on her own when she was at the Beaux-Arts in Paris a short time after the war, an etching that lay there in the basement among other works, all just as beautiful, that Paula's savage hand had almost entirely destroyed.

§

And at this hour she should have been dancing alone on the dance floor in that stream of shadows where each dancer performed her own obstinate dance between the dawn and the morning, thought Johnie as she waited for Lynda, immobile at the window, who could know, perhaps Lynda would come back, as she had so many times before, once she felt repentant. But time was passing —

long, morose, empty hours — and Lynda still did not appear, eyes red with shame. By an inconceivable cruelty of fate, thought Johnie, she might not return at all this time, that was the insane side of love, our sentiments are as perishable as we are ourselves. "Ingrate," murmured Johnie, lighting a cigarette, observing with disgust the trembling of her hands, "and for a man, no less." And for Johnie, Lynda's pointy high-heeled pumps that capsized on the icy sidewalks were united with the thought of the other fall, Lynda's one true degradation that had seduced all men, the grandfather, the uncle, the brother, the brother-in-law; yes, in her deplorable candor Lynda had always consented to their brutal touch, even taken pleasure in it. Lynda came back from the office at night — it was useless to try to direct her back to her studies, she didn't apply herself, she promised to study law one day, but that was just a dream — the heavy odors of men's wool garments, a bouquet of damnable smells, thought Johnie, the cigars they smoked, the hairy pelt that covered their musculature (Johnie took pleasure in loving only those young people that looked like gods and growing tired of them before seven in the morning), intoxicating poisons from those bodies groomed to seize and deflower Lynda. "Don't be discouraged, Johnie, one day I'll finish criminal law. Meanwhile I type all day for my boss and I'm so tired." "Tired at sixteen," muttered Johnie, incredulous. And Lynda would stretch out next to Johnie, wheedling even after she had fallen asleep. Perhaps, thought Johnie, she was bored with the prisoner she put to sleep every night before going to dance at the Club ... When she didn't fall asleep right away, Lynda opened her wide eyes, brown eyes of a shifting purity in which Johnie read a faint submissiveness — what point was there in suffering if Lynda betrayed her confidence — she would go to Abeille's where there was always Gérard, with the black curls of her hair, spring flowers before the arrival of springtime, Abeille, Thérèse, Doudouline, Polydor. A shame, Johnie would say to herself, that Lynda should sleep alone in that wanton pose, receptive to the pleasures she had known during the day! Lynda was just as guilty also of luring Johnie away from her desk at the university where she was so at home, far from Austria which should have been her destination. Johnie had drifted with Lynda over the highways of North America, biking, hitchhiking, and while the sky and the trees spun themselves out, she and Lynda had acquired all those useless skills, cartomancy, astrology, leaving her essay, her novel that she had sped away from in a drawer she would not open again until much later. Her knapsack on her long, straight, fragile back that supported her occasionally rounded shoulders, Johnie had followed Lynda over the roads to the confines of a world that was lit too brightly by the sun, where, suffocating with the heat, she had begged Lynda to find "a place to sleep, a river to wash in, a hotel with a shower ..." while Lynda, always brimming with resources and health, collected, in a place where there had been no one before, on a beach, along a footpath, in a grove of wild roses like in the desert, a troop of men, and often found the hotel that Johnie had been looking for with the last of her strength. Johnie could not imagine the awe those men felt around Lynda, following her everywhere, and her humble tarot cards, men that Johnie, a wave of heat drying out her eyes, hadn't seen on the burning land. They were either dressed all in white, with white straw tourist's hats, or barely dressed at all in the motley of the beaches and the undergrowth of the forest; they would spring up from behind a bush or a tree, wading in a stream, and then Lynda docilely went back to the road with Johnie, the fire in her eyes seemed to have been appeased, and Johnie was overcome by doubt — was Lynda living off of prostitution, drugs? — and resigned herself to the incoherence of her destiny, the love of danger in which Lynda took as much pleasure as fear, walking only in those clumps of trees that smelled of snakes, climbing only those mountains where the forest ranger, the ferocious beast, the bird of prey, the venomous insect could be roaming around. Johnie pushed her way ahead on the dry stones of those clearings, those woods, and climbed the mountains where the wild animals roamed, her knapsack weighing heavy on her shoulder blades. "Your poor back must hurt so much, I'll give you a massage tonight," Lynda would say tenderly, and in the still of the evening when they knelt down by the fire, Johnie impatiently awaited that happy moment when Lynda's caresses became expert, a balm on her hidden wounds, she thought, while Lynda's hands, the fingernails polished and filed too sharp, were involuntarily cruel, descending slowly, voluptuously on her battered back.

Johnie opened the window and leaned out over the street into the soft time of twilight. The two students, girls who lived across the street, were coming back from the Club on their bicycles and holding hands, fingers locked together, but the gripping bond of their fingers, the approach of the bicycles rolling over the asphalt in the glowing light that was brighter during that season than the light of summer, tortured Johnie, who would even have preferred that spring not return that year, much less those girls laughing and whispering in the vegetal dust the tires of their bicycles stirred up in the street. Soon the airplanes leaving for vacation would streak across the sky. With a melancholy heart, Johnie would watch those impetuous silver arrows on the horizon — like the students' bicycles on the asphalt and its golden reflections, or the razor in Lynda's bedroom and her escape with a man — all of that tapestry of movement that had so quickly shaken the spheres of Johnie's world held a conjuration of the divine order, she thought, like the stars that generated our miseries from birth till death. Yes, that had to be how the will of God expressed itself, thought Johnie, revolted, and everything that belonged to the divine order, like a star falling on the roof of the earth, cut off and shattered our lives. Even without faith you could imitate Polydor who bowed beneath the yoke of God, for there was no choice but to obey the rules that were laid out far away from man, and to understand that the evolution of a thought, that was it, a malediction in motion that with one headstrong movement, broke the often calm, sometimes comfortable relationship that Johnie had with herself. Suddenly, inoffensively, the girls across the street had chained their bicycles to a tree, they had a garden they would cultivate that summer, they had painted their little house in pink and grey before the end of winter, and they were going to love each other for a year, two years, a lifetime, thought Johnie, unaware of the fact that God, on a whim, because somewhere he had set himself in motion, had just abandoned Johnie to the irony of her fate.

And barely awake, Doudouline was singing or recounting her dreams, her round, graceful hand describing in the dry air of the bedroom the landscapes she had seen, trees of a deep brown or a somber mauve, their texture as rich and supple as velvet, the crystal pools she'd bathed in, prudently interrupting her own narrative — and she knew Polydor's irritated glance from beneath her bushy eyebrows all too well — to ask in an abrupt morning tone, "Why is there so much sugar in my coffee?" And the incantation in multiple octaves that Doudouline had begun upon waking came to a close, for she would soon start talking about the music she was writing for her rock opera. Too much sugar in the coffee, too much syrup on the pancakes, since Doudouline had been on a diet life was a torment, no one in that house could eat normally anymore, and after relating her pagan dreams and humming the tune of a song she intended to write, Doudouline, no longer entitled to Sunday indulgences, the hot croissants that Polydor served her in bed, seemed disappointed at being there with Polydor, who was reading St. John of the Cross in Abeille's living room, where it was always too hot or too cold or too dry because the thermostat never worked. "I'm going to call Mother and borrow her car," she cried suddenly. Doudouline worried Polydor, a Doudouline who would become too thin, Polydor thought, for the day she would sing at the Animal Fabuleux, the nightclub where she gave her concerts, guided by her mother's advice on the theater — she certainly could stand to lose a few pounds, as Sophie suggested with pleasant courtesy, but this way she would look like a freak — Doudouline was so delicate and sensitive, though, that she was touched by any manifestation of kindness or tenderness, even if, as Doudouline claimed, Sophie had seemed a bit too sure of herself when she said that about her daughter. Perhaps she could order fewer pizzas, less barbecued chicken — that food wasn't healthy — lose a bit of weight, but not too much. Already Polydor was having trouble recognizing her — less sugar in her coffee! Doudouline was becoming an ascetic, and a woman who didn't eat was a woman of no desires, thought Polydor, and Doudouline, lighter every day — this was the other worry — was already flying off to the city to find Abeille and bring her back to the house, in Sophie's green car with the top down below the blue sky, the cold more agreeable than the springtime. That shadow was there, thought Doudouline, Sophie had attacked her daughter that day — "You call me all the time, as if I didn't have enough of that with my playwright, do you know what it is to work with those creatures, you should think of your father, I'm going to hang up on you, you're unbearable, now you want more money? How much? You're going to bankrupt me, listen, don't forget batteries for your show, for the bass and the guitar ...." Poor Mother, she's so nervous, thought Doudouline, all I was doing was telling her my dreams, but as Polydor often pointed out to her, her feelings for her mother were too devout, but this did not disturb the chaotic equilibrium of the world, Doudouline thought, for, despite everything, there *was* a tenacious equilibrium that endured throughout the worst catastrophes, while she, Doudouline, was born to sing, not the apocalyptic rock that Abeille listened to with her headphones, but a music at once expressive and ethereal that floated in a stream of tell-tale images toward the year 2000. No one knew who Doudouline was yet, with the possible exception of her mother, despite that sour pursing of her lips when she said to her daughter, "God, you're irritating," or "So when *is* Abeille's show? When are you girls going to stop dreaming?" And now Doudouline was driving through the city, refraining from running over pedestrians — kill off a few of those and the equilibrium of the world would not be disturbed — and Abeille, with her stories of men and parks, even if she had learned judo and karate, was sure to be found one day in a green garbage bag. Doudouline flushed hot, it was like the day that Sophie had told her that her haircut, Doudouline's blond hair, was all wrong, with that unfathomable smile she wore when she spoke of Doudouline's faults — she did have a few good qualities too — and that brother of hers, the monarch of passivity who spent his life smoking and vegetating in a hammock in the Antilles while his slaves waved fans to cool his skin, who did he think he was, Gauguin? Polydor had kissed and coddled her all night, and a pleasant warmth washed over Doudouline. If what her mother said was true, she had a crazy talent — *was* what her mother said true? — but in the world of show business there was nothing more precarious, she had lived in communes all her life — artists' communes with her mother where she ran about in the nude not only in the fields but on the sidewalks as well, following the example set by Sophie and whatever provisional father happened to be there. Today, the commune of girls, much as she hated that passé word — "gang" was better. ("But to you, Doudouline, with your French grandmother in Poitiers, such words are forbidden, cherubic one-year-old superstar that you were in TV commercials for baby soap.") It was a shame that her mother was so untrusting, but, despite the sudden harsh silence or the sound of Sophie grinding her teeth on the phone, the equilibrium of the world, so precarious itself, was maintained, since Doudouline hadn't yet had any major accidents with Sophie's car that she gunned past the pedestrians, the roof open to the glory of the day, for she, Doudouline, was living and breathing and in love with Polydor, in love.

§

And on that day, perhaps, Johnie, who liked to go off
without Lynda — as it was necessary, she thought, to be
free of Lynda's scorpions in the African sand dunes, her
hash joints, her insects that she crushed in the palm of her
hand, and her experiments with the opium pipe that night
in the hunter's tent — though she was sick of traveling
and disgusted with layover airports where she waited
barely awake in the dawn's greyness that did not dissipate
with the arrival of the day — had carried her personal,
though, she thought, hardly unique misery to the blazing
sun of an English isle, perhaps she would be inspired by
that unheard-of laziness, by those places of privilege
where people lay yawning in chaise longues, among
leaves and trees, by the sea, and finally have the courage
to write, even though Radclyffe Hall, called John by her
lover in the intimacy of daily life, and the flame of her
genius seemed farther and farther away, as if suddenly she
were no more than a phantom, not even the fragile John,
long imprisoned with the ambiguity of her virtues and
singular qualities in a woman's body, that Johnie bore a
tender devotion for. Johnie reached up a finger to touch
her downy earrings, a gift from Lynda that stirred up all
her memories, Lynda had been loving and generous with
this gift of a bit of wire and a sea gull feather, Lynda who
could be dead now but had once adorned and decorated
Johnie, while Johnie was now roaming a golf course, not
trembling a bit, thinking about the rush of Lynda's adventure and her audacity, pursuing a woman in white shorts

that she had spotted during a dinner, out of boredom, and wanting to invite her for a cocktail on one of the flowery terraces that overlooked the sea. Lynda by preference would have chosen a man, like that old judge from California she'd brought into her chambers, but Johnie did not like that reversal of ethical values that had for so long determined Lynda's conduct; the woman in white shorts, because she too was bored — she had a husband in Palm Springs, a private plane, a second home and three greyhounds — was especially susceptible to Johnie's aggressiveness as she disdainfully moistened her lips in her piña colada: It would have been so easy to seduce the millionaire's wife, to suspend that plump, frightened body in its own sensations, inject that tranquil flesh with flame, but Johnie, timid herself, ended up alone in her hotel room, the prismatic reflections of a carafe of water multiplying off the mirror and the glass of the carafe as the sun sank entirely into the sea. It was so quiet in the room, thought Johnie, that she could hear every one of her heartbeats.

§

Abeille was drawing and painting in the humidity of the stone walls that housed Paula's engravings, below the fetid dripping of melted snow that soaked the basement. With a fervent pen she created storms of ink — "as if she were Victor Hugo on his island," Paula said in a hoarse voice that was suddenly vibrant with emotion — everything that proceeded feverishly from her imagination that she tried to explain to herself, decapitated heads against landscapes of mountains and plains, dead birds with their beaks open; this was the picture of her isolation on the earth, she thought. The disappearance of a beloved being leaves us with these unfinished, troubling images: For a long time our souls were heavy with the debris of these things, living beings that had left us, and we'd see their image in the external world, suddenly deformed and nightmarish. "But that's too morbid," said Paula as if she were Abeille's master, whipping her, "Why not be more simple?" Paula often came back from the theater short of breath, blind to everything around her, checking the irregularity of her breathing with one hand over her heart, she who wouldn't quit smoking and would light up again as soon as her respiration was a bit calmer — what was truly morbid, thought Abeille, was Paula's respiratory catastrophes, her cough and the brownish liquid she spat up that so frightened Abeille. "No one lives forever and I don't like old age," Paula said putting her white choirboy blouse back on, her outfit for painting as well as for making love to a woman, thought Abeille, and Paula went down, in a silence that was uniquely hers, menacing, sulky, sometimes a bit sinister, to the moonlit chasm of the basement where she maneuvered her plates of yellow ochre and black inks beneath the trembling light bulb that hung by a wire from a beam of the ceiling. For in the basement, surrounded by her etchings, Paula was rarely joyous, even if Abeille could not stop telling her how much she admired her work. "Oh, be quiet," Paula would groan, "You say that just to please me, like my mother who kept all the reviews from the papers; I didn't discover that until after her death ... You know there's no future here for art that is still genuine, authentic." Paula's humor only surfaced in the kitchen, like the bed, where she was always serene, the kitchen was a sacred place of ritual where Paula, in keeping with the traditions her mother had bequeathed to her, devoted herself to transforming food into a celebration, where Abeille was permitted to eat sitting at her end of the table. Paula pushed in her chair so that she wouldn't get the idea to escape to her house or to the Club where she would dance all night and see Thérèse again, who she should not be seeing: Paula got out the holiday tablecloth, embroidered with lace and pearls, the work of her mother, she said, and the subtlety of the embroidery on the sheets, like on Paula's lingerie — she leapt with intrepid allure in her silk panties as if she were preparing to mount a horse, thought Abeille — always threw Paula into nostalgic reveries, for Paula's mother lived on everywhere, in the flood of manual daintiness, the tablecloth she unfolded from a drawer, or a pillow with designs copied from childhood desires that concealed a dog or a cat. The fingers of fairies had left their subtle and generous marks there, and, as she bowed her head over her steaming bowl of stew, Abeille could feel the presence of that mother whose memory was purified, glorified, a woman above reproach; Abeille had also had a mother who had already disappeared and heard the notes unfurling from her piano when she played in the afternoon. An emaciated hand, almost the reflection of a hand, turned the pages of her music score. The dead are with us, thought Abeille, begging us to keep them intact in our memory even as we blot them out little by little, and now Paula was talking about things that were so far behind her, she said, so far in her past, the first showings of her etchings in Paris, her friends that had committed suicide, Gilles who had been found hanging in a courtroom at the age of twenty, Madeleine who had let her gas stove asphyxiate her in Europe ... And Abeille listened to the song of exhaustion and desolation that rose from Paula's chest and thought also of Doudouline, Polydor, Johnie, and the carefree thoughtlessness that sometimes seemed to be guiding them toward their futures, and it was the time of deception when, back when she was still at home, Abeille would watch Thérèse put her skis away and hang her sneakers around her neck by their laces after her treks up the mountain. The time of lying when Thérèse purred over her cup of coffee as if she had never meant to leave, when, with her benevolent, comprehensive smile, she was already revealing to Abeille the unease of an imminent break, this unease expressed itself in a cold melancholy that they felt when they were next to each other, among the cushions on the bed where Abeille would come to surprise Thérèse, who had her nose in a book — it would sometimes occur to her to raise that statuesque nose to look at Abeille, but most often Thérèse read those boring volumes of philosophy that Polydor brought back for her from the library for hours, flat on her stomach, her ample form squashing the mattress — a melancholy that was also in the air. The heat was so low in the bedroom that when she exhaled hard Abeille could see her breath frozen before her, and thus the infectious sadness won them over, and Abeille told Thérèse about her visits to the sex shops with Gérard — at any cost, she had to revive Thérèse's eroticism, shock her with bawdy details — and Thérèse, who was reading Marcus Aurelius to better understand Polydor (what good was it to try to understand someone in that dusty house where the walls and the ceiling were falling into ruin?), suddenly cried with anger that seemed justified to her, "Sex shops, is it now? When are you girls going to stop wasting your time? How shameful, how degrading — sex shops!"

§

Paula was opening another bottle of rosé, and, in the dust of another life, in the chandelier's incandescent light that flowed over the tablecloth and the part in Paula's hair, Abeille again saw Thérèse smiling at her before leaving for the university in the morning, her books under her arm, or stretched out on her back among her many pillows, as if she were posing for Goya, naked in the confined light of the winter she was emerging from, so vast, on her lips that smile of mocking tenderness that Abeille had painted. Abeille listened to Paula's hoarse voice as she continued her colorless monologue — after her overindulgence in food and wine she meticulously wiped the corners of her mouth with her left hand, without unfolding her napkin from its pyramid; Paula's fingerprints on the white of the tablecloth increased the sensation of being possessed that Abeille felt so often with Paula, or her neurasthenia when Abeille was separated from the girls of the group for several days. "You're already thinking about going out while I'm preparing filet mignon for you," said Paula, offended. "Fine, tomorrow night, if you want ...."

At the theater, as well as at restaurants, Paula resurrected her elegant manners, "manners like her father, the good doctor," said Madame Boudreau, who never seemed to notice Paula's fingers, greasy with brown sauce, on the tablecloth, "the good education your mother gave you, forbidding you and your sisters to move in your chair or talk when we went on vacation all together in a hotel —

yes, can you imagine, what luxury, a hotel! And your dear mother, may she rest in peace, who loved you so much called you her son." A wild, carnivorous animal, thought Abeille, that fed on other animals, the lamb, the steer, the pig. They couldn't graze in a pasture in peace without Paula, her mouth watering, thinking about preying upon them. In society she was a woman of almost timid docility, sitting up straight in her chair, as she had been taught in the hotels over summer vacations, during the era of the wire-rimmed glasses on her beaky nose, when the doctor cut the meat on her plate, built cathedrals of piled-up potatoes to rouse his daughter Paula's appetite, Paula who was also her mother's son, an idea to which the whole family was reconciled, Madame Boudreau said. When she went out, her hair was so clean it shone, Paula's hair was a somber chestnut brown, revived — oiled, you might say — by rollers and brush, it had such a romantic allure in its iridescence and elasticity that you understood immediately that Paula belonged to another epoch, that she was incapable of liking pop music, videos, Madonna and the others; Paula, with her strips of hair that covered her cheeks, her long, severe nose, her strong, sometimes vindictive chin, her voice often low and resentful, had a past, and a past was the prolonging of old sufferings woven into her nerves, while for Abeille, the pleasure of being in the world was the coursing of all those nerves under her skin, that fast, poisonous excitation of the blood in her veins, whether you were making love, dancing at the Club, taking heedless pleasure in a passing instant — it was the future, so mysterious it was, that pulled you forward. A past that wasn't there could not devastate you yet, and the future. Abeille's happiness was now as she ate oysters with Paula, drank muscadet, a Paula at last refined who didn't swallow her egg raw, as she did at home, or lick the bottoms of her saucepans with an uncertain tongue, and now held herself straight and proud, savored the tender, full-flavored flesh of her mollusks with calm lubricity. Then, leaning over the street — for Paula only liked restaurants that were high up — Abeille had noticed Doudouline gliding along the sidewalk in her silk scarf; she climbed the iron spiral staircase with a winged step and came to lean on Abeille's shoulder, placing her rosy, radiant face close to Abeille's as if to kiss her. She had already gotten too thin, thought Abeille, and this gave her a new sophistication, almost an arrogance, especially when she went out in her mother's convertible. Paula looked at those ruffled heads — what was that kind of hairstyle called, she wondered. Someone was sure to tell her that was Art Nouveau, Doudouline's ridiculous hair — and what did her mother think of it? — drawn up like arrows woven into her head. Abeille, however, didn't seem to find anything abnormal in Doudouline's behavior. Paula looked at their heads now so close together, in conspiratorial chatter, you ran into the girls of the group everywhere. With one swipe of her sovereign hand, Paula had swept everything off the table, tipped over the wine and oysters onto Abeille's feet, forgetting in her rage her solemn public etiquette. Art Nouveau, that they're trying to tell me about, I was there long before them, and Doudouline's mother, too, working away at Strindberg — who knew Strindberg here? — going to perform his plays in France. Since then, familiarity with foreign writers had become a snobbism. Paula inhaled deeply, catching her breath, and amid all this havoc Doudouline smiled with an impenetrable air, holding her dirtied silk scarf with her fingertips, and Paula thought of the magnificent sets she had constructed for an opera or a theater piece that were dead before dawn, disintegrated like cardboard boxes someone had kicked along a rainy sidewalk, she thought. Her mother was right, the only art she was worthy of was etching; there was always that charred black tree in the basement, and, then, there had been forty people in the audience to see Wagner — today, of course, people flattered themselves that they liked Wagner and reserved tickets months in advance — and now those girls with the safety pins in their ears try to explain to me what art is, but Doudouline was already disappearing towards the street and Abeille watched Paula's white teeth in the black of the night in fascination, their savage gleam that hypnotized Abeille, though she was suddenly afraid of a woman who ate shellfish that were still alive, pigs, calves that had barely been born, and lambs, devouring them in her mind even before they had been killed and were grazing innocently in the fields and on the island of women at rest, who spent their lives, often alone, divided between their chaise longues and the sea, surrounded by a continuous parade of black servants, each in their turn, the chauffeurs, the gardeners, the masseurs.

Johnie gained access to the social circles that were forbidden to her when she was with the girls in the group — after all, she couldn't live with them twenty-four hours a day, they were too demanding, Gérard especially, ever since she had thrown herself into the South American hash trade — and the doors of grand hotels opened for Johnie, castles and sun rooms she went back to at night, along walkways strewn with white pebbles, into the arms of an occasionally mature woman, a promenade of loose sensuality that Lynda would have embellished with her teasing, while Johnie felt so awkward with the woman she was escorting, her sandals sinking into the moss of the eucalyptus forests that surrounded those ponds where the swans and pink flamingos cooed, the days and the hours be fore nighttime flowed together like a convalescence, under the yellow sun, in a wicker chair from which Johnie could barely get up in the heat to smoke a cigarette or observe Marianne or one or another of those filthy rich married women who were languorously attentive (because they were alone) to the weakness in Johnie's soul that called out to them hoping not to be heard, for it was the future polyglot in her that loved their groans enrobed in light British accents, strong Dutch and German accents. Johnie listened, sometimes caught a glance from one of them from beneath the parasols that only half-protected them, their eyes were barely open under the shadows of their hats, under the dappled shadows cast by their parasols and straw hats where their blue or green eyes seemed to have been creased by an enigmatic patience: Life had given them all it had to offer and they had nothing to look forward to. Johnie, meanwhile, dragged her slimmed-down body towards the waves — when she had been with Lynda on that island, she thought, she had been so healthy — but it was doubtlessly better to waste away peacefully, in the slightly idle, slightly drunken laxity of that island, that bath of conventional pleasures where the faults of Johnie's indolence — laziness, Thérèse would have said, whether you get up in the morning or go to sleep then, you're always tired and languishing, circles under your eyes — only weighed heavier upon her: perhaps by not sleeping alone she hoped to replace the ghost of Lynda on the empty pillow, in the bed where Johnie had seen her camp out more often than sleep, sitting Indian style with her cigarettes and the submarine sandwiches she ate half of and then threw out with the corrosive ashes of her hash joints — but there had been so much clarity in that disorder while here the order was of a troubled clarity, despite the sun, it was evident that Johnie did not belong to that world of women whose respectability, no matter what they did, was preserved incorruptibly intact. All was nothing but lies, the air they breathed, too intoxicating for her sickness, the hot, shining sea that swept over her slight frame like a wave of cold, the women whose eyes were blue or green diamonds, under their parasols, could transform their gazes into hard, glinting weapons, for Johnie had no protection against those women who were all capable of betraying her. Lynda had entwined her too fragile body around the imperfect skeleton of Johnie's back, Gérard had hidden her face in the thick curls of her hair against that back, but on that island nothing could be seen of Johnie but her exaggeratedly long neck, the nervous curve taken by her shoulders when her body had grown too fast; Johnie touched her bare stomach where Lynda's head so often took refuge, and suddenly, there would be no mischievous invasion in that bed upon the white, anemic girl's stomach in the sun, a hollow space that recalled Gérard's stomach when she strode through the corridors of Abeille's house, such a solitary nudity in the white of winter that delivered punishment outdoors and shed a pale greenish light over Gérard that fell onto her cheeks when she stood at the window and lifted the hem of her Mickey Mouse T-shirt in her idleness. If Johnie were to identify with the animal world, she could compare herself to the shorebirds, the ones that had survived the storm, they too were long in the leg and had curved spines, and God had burdened them at birth with an extreme delicacy that matched Johnie's in her dealings with the earth. Even in their infinite tininess, they were quite robust and survived the hurricane, the tempest, with their beaks buried in the algae they fell back onto the mirror of the water. God in his love for them, in return for their submissiveness, their steadfast obedience to the laws of his creation, had endowed them with a tremendous strength, so why couldn't Johnie herself submit to the demands of her fate like those humble creatures? At first, when she got off the boat onto the island, Johnie had lived in one of the cabanas in the brush, as if she were still with Lynda and ready for adventure, but far from Lynda, she wilted, not bothering to eat or sleep, while the fire stretched over the sea; one morning two black maids had driven her out, shaking the sweat-drenched sheets, the pillows, and the mattress, in which Johnie was starting to mildew with the humidity. But in that privileged corner of the island she was appreciated, an object coveted by those women, they saw in her some incendiary ambiguity that they would never have dared to express to their husbands or lovers but here exposed to the burning air, throwing away the defenses and prejudices they had guarded severely at home with their formalities. On an island where there were so many blacks, did Johnie also have the right to exist? It was sad that life had seemed so empty to her. Then her eyes lit upon one of the bodies floating supine in the sea, come, as she had, from elsewhere and caressed by the waves, the man in the yellow and red checked bathing suit planted his head in the sand, his beached body, inert for long hours, warming the Nordic glacier that everyone carried with them in the winter in those sandy lairs, Johnie reflected, suddenly inclined to mercy in the face of such simplicity. "If Lynda were to come back I'd forgive her everything," she thought, there next to the water's sparkling reflections, the sea that had held her in a vise-like grip for weeks. Johnie could neither return from it nor escape it, she was so weak, but there she could touch time, time that occupied a concrete nothingness between the water and the sky and the permanence of their light, all that time during which Johnie was living in a somber passivity, exhausted, though, by each second as if by an eternity of bravery and endurance. There she was, not reading any books, not writing to her friends, but, like the man immobile in the sand, eroded by the water a bit more each day, time was dragging her with its powerful lures towards her death, along with the sleeping tourist and his big red nose buried in the grains of sand. Then at that instant a yacht broke into a crazy race, plowing through much foam, and Johnie saw a girl, very young and half-naked, laughing in the middle of a group of boys: it was a bright, cheerful laugh, indifferent to the calamities that filled Johnie's soul, Lynda's laugh, the look of her tanned, exposed chest in a tableau that rode along the sea leaving a silvery wake, and Johnie trembled at feeling her so near, though that slim figure evaporating into a blue fog was not Lynda and the strident laugh that burst from Lynda's white teeth was not actually hers but more visceral, thought Johnie, but in the eternity of that island where every second was weighted with sorrow, Johnie had brought Lynda back to her side, on a pleasure boat in Greece, linked the smell of brine and the wind to that face as it fled, heard the clarity of Lynda's laugh, Lynda the salesgirl hiding in the dark of her mother's boutique, the mother who had taken her coughing, urban-born child far away to warm countries, whose laugh on that boat had been an eruption of pure joy. Then Johnie turned abruptly toward the shore where a woman was whistling for her poodle and for the "boy" who was bringing her a screwdriver on a platter, and although Johnie was conscious of the fact that that whistle was also meant for her, as Marianne had already invited her to play languid games with the men before she went out for the night, she saw nothing of Marianne but a smile hidden beneath her wide-brimmed hat and the shade of her parasol and sneered upon associating with a woman of such a powerful race, even if that slightly haughty character bore a resemblance to Virginia Woolf, which had first seduced her. She had looked at Marianne's head bowed nobly toward her while at her feet — but perhaps that was it, thought Johnie, a position of servility that was pleasing to a woman like Marianne — recognizing the elongated sentences that charmed her when she read a book, the elegance of a language that seemed to come right out of literature, when Marianne spoke, and suddenly, that voice that had entranced Johnie for hours, the voice of Marianne, who was not Virginia Woolf but did call her characters to mind, had emitted a whistle, a come-hither command that invited Johnie to partake in late-afternoon caresses by the pool: God, therefore, had come back into Johnie's life with Lynda's departure, even if Johnie didn't believe in God and never gave the matter any thought, God appeared when there was confusion or suffering. It was a sign, and since an obscure divinity was infiltrating Johnie's life, she wanted to know what debasement she would be dragged to, though perhaps she would know nothing yet but the pangs of shame and the dull ache of disgust, disgust that rankled within her as she stroked Marianne's friends' backs with her peace-giving hands slathered with suntan lotion by the pool: Johnie was reminded of a crew of ship-

wrecked survivors dreaming blissfully on their rubber
rafts, and it seemed to her that the satisfied complaisance
of their bodies deserved to be punished, so little did each
aristocratic head at the end of a supine back think about its
own mortality. A tuft of gray hair, stuck with perspiration
to the nape of one of their necks, beneath the stripes of her
bath towel, rendered Johnie's disgust even more acute, she
was thinking that she could turn into that woman one day,
all attributes of youth lost, warming her self like this for
one last hedonistic summer in wintertime. She reproached
herself also for those skimpy carnal links that had nothing
to do with the reality of her life. By living clandestinely a
life that was not clandestine for her, that she was used to
living out in the open, she was betraying the girls of the
group and their plainness, their frankness, with her lying
and hypocrisy. Abeille doubtlessly would have told her
that her literary attractions were nothing but lures, that
her story of a resemblance to Virginia Woolf was actually
the price of a perfume scented on Marianne's throat or in
the pleats of her silk blouses as Johnie rummaged through
her drawers that Johnie had become infatuated with, as if
she were still excited, in the innate decadence she'd in-
herited from the social class she belonged to by virtue of
wealth; no, she was losing her soul here, Doudouline, who
lived only for her music, would have said. Suddenly,
Johnie separated herself from Marianne, as if she had been
her captive. In a phone booth from which she could see
the sun setting over the sea, Johnie waited, collapsing, for
Lynda's voice, her breath, and inhaled the persistent odor
of acacia, which sadly reminded her that she had drunk
too much of that rum punch the night before with
Marianne. She had fallen into an acacia bush, only to be
gathered up against Marianne's chest, while Marianne

laughed in her white dress. Anyway, she drank too much, as Thérèse had often told her: "Anyone who calls you at ten in the morning will hear the clink of ice cubes in your glass." And now, tired of that very drunkenness, Johnie was waiting for the voice that crossed oceans to tell her that her world was no longer adrift, that they were waiting for her at the house, but she heard only Lynda's voice, all the charm of its insolence gone from that mechanically pronounced, neutralized message, for Johnie had taught her "not to be too whiny, even on the telephone," the voice that she herself had purged of lyricism, that flatly mumbled this message: "You have reached Johnie and Lynda's place. We're not home right now ... At the tone ... You have reached Johnie and Lynda's place ..." That murmuring had agitated the air, Johnie and Lynda, Lynda and Johnie — yes, they had gone out, but would be back soon, and you could hear Lynda's running, impatient steps on the wooden stairs of the apartment, the distinct sound of Lynda's pointy high-heeled pumps as they climbed. The murmured message, therefore, announced more than Johnie and Lynda's absence; it announced their disappearance, for neither one was there, in the home where they had lived in such unison, though one telephone call could still mingle their destinies. Lynda's murmur, not addressed to anyone, like the laugh of the girl on her yacht with her bare torso, thought Johnie, had stirred up the air like a cyclone, and without a doubt this was done by divine will, although Johnie felt so oppressed during the long silence that had followed Lynda's message on the answering machine. The air, despite everything, the sky, the blue water, all around her was inexorably light, the water-skiing heroes still flying high in the sky, snagged by the string of a multi-colored balloon that followed their curve across the azure, with the birds and the airplanes, as if the torments of life and love were affairs belonging to another world, as perhaps they were, thought Johnie, suddenly recalling the razor on the bedside table in the bedroom she shared with Lynda, the white bear's head rug onto which she had spitefully dropped ash from her cigarette, and that ancient object whose cruelty was fresh in her memory, Gérard's cap. Each of these meteors had come from another planet; with its allotment of affliction and shadows, didn't it chase all the light from the island? But the air was delicious, an orchestra of young musicians was playing calypso under the trees, and Virginia Woolf, a book in her hand, was walking toward Johnie, for at that instant it could only be her, controlling water and the ashes of higher minds in the night, it was her and her wide-brimmed hat in the diffuse light, and, for getting that she was cold, Johnie ran to Marianne, feeling all of her awkwardness in that one gesture — you only saw that in movies , and even then, only with men — and bent down and kissed her hand. Although the air was whirling with all these cyclones, the phosphorescence and agility of the island seemed unshakable; three ice cubes were melting in the glass of vodka that Marianne held in her hand and this, except for a small brown female cat that had bounded out from the foliage where she had been sleeping all day to attack a sea gull, stop the beating of its heart and tear off its wings with one swift, hungry bite, was the only movement, the only stirring: Marianne had placed her book down on the white marble table, the pages turned by themselves in the hot evening wind, in the strange melody of her voice she spoke to Johnie who listened, suddenly impressed by the refinement of all her gestures — even if all she was doing was lifting a hand to her eyes to shield them from the sun as it set over the sea — about those periods in the life of a philosopher or an artist when inspiration was barren, when for a long time "nothing that was alive happened." To hear her as she penetrated to the heart of a genius' distress (she was talking about Schopenhauer, whose biography she was reading), you would have thought she had lived in intimacy with the somber philosopher, thought Johnie. By what diabolical intuition did Marianne broach that subject, at that moment, during that period when Johnie's life was neither good nor inspired, when an imperturbable nothingness had installed itself. The three ice cubes had melted at the bottom of the glass, which was sweating out pearly drops, the little brown cat had disappeared with its bloody prey into the bushes, and Johnie told herself that she must have misjudged Marianne, confused her too quickly with her group of frivolous companions, their idleness almost a crime, roasting in the sun all day, playing tennis or golf, showing their boyish white underpants. Marianne had to be an unusual woman, beneath her dry, haughty appearances, to enjoy the company of someone like Johnie, who had not read Schopenhauer herself, and perhaps Marianne was not so haughty — it occurred to her to go for walks on the beach, holding the arm of her black chauffeur, and to visit his family, bringing gifts as if she had long been familiar with the island, aware of the obligations of privilege. And yet, when a servant came to give her massages in the morning, Johnie, contemplating Marianne's muscular, still juvenile body, naked and almost motionless on the massage table, as if it had been stripped of its life, in its rosy, bronze majesty, Johnie despised the bizarre ritual in which, with the most prudent friction, the beautiful servile hands, kneading her flesh like wax, could have delivered a mutinous stab, especially when the masseur's fingers ran dreamily over the lines of her neck. Marianne, who had been somnolent, woke suddenly with a loud moan: "You're hurting me," she said softly, and repeated these words to Johnie, "Why do you keep talking about leaving soon? I can't have an intelligent conversation with anyone here but you ... You're hurting me ...." Or she would say, in a voice that hid her chagrin, "You're going to hurt me. Girls your age don't know what they're doing ...." But now Marianne was talking about Schopenhauer, her refinement was immense, thought Johnie, she owned many galleries of paintings in New York, her refinement and her wealth, while Johnie owned nothing, except for that credit card of her father's that she had abused too much already, and she was so uneducated, in her idleness with the girls of the group, she hadn't read Schopenhauer yet, much less made a single philosophical discovery, except for her pessimism. She was one of those creatures "for whom, for long periods of time, nothing happened," and that thought seemed so unbearable to her that she abruptly announced to Marianne once again that she ought to be returning, that a friend was nervously waiting for her at the house, and bit by bit she let herself be carried away by false hopes: if Marianne's limpid eyes darkened below her wide-brimmed hat — "No, you can't leave, I'll keep you here" — Johnie's eyes shone with a moist glow, for Marianne, in the precious education Johnie would receive, would have wanted her to reflect along with Schopenhauer, cure her laziness, and Johnie felt, as if it were irreversible, the weight of those days when, for so long, alone or with the girls of the group, even if she was advancing closer to death each day, nothing happened, nothing happened.

§

And now Gérard was leaning toward the blue lamp,
above the rays that the candles scattered from their glass
holders, she looked at the older women covering their
nostrils with one hand — like her, they had worked all
night at the Club — for them the ceremony of discreet
sniffing was already beginning, the almost silent aspira-
tion of powder spread out on cigarette papers, and even if
this rite was hardly a habit for her — she'd only smoked
hash with the girls of the group, but since she'd been selling it, she thought, it was no longer enough — she would
show them all what she was capable of, and she shivered
from head to toe as her cheeks reddened slightly beneath
the black curls of her hair. Polydor and Doudouline were
sure to be asleep at this hour, and as for Abeille, she
wasn't there to torment Gérard with her reprimands:
"What, you're snorting cocaine, Gérard, before this it was
pills you took to go to sleep, others you took to wake up,
speed, what's it going to be tomorrow, are you going to
shoot poison into your veins?" And Johnie had fled to her
far-away islands for a woman, as would probably happen
frequently, and rather than grumbling to herself in her
empty, lonely bed or kicking her plastic slippers against
the wall, Gérard thought it was time that she be initiated
into life's tougher experiences, time to come out of the
cocoon of her whole dreamy, sleepy existence, an
unformed butterfly that would quickly burn in the flame
of drugs — some of her friends had started earlier, in
school, she thought, with mushrooms and acid, it was

time for her to be respected, and the other girls at the bar, even the youngest ones, were all on coke — but they barely noticed Gérard, the girls didn't say anything, their attention focused elsewhere — and Gérard would have liked to hear how brave she was, taking the risk of joining a clan that seemed threatening to her — bowing their heads heavily forward over the bluish light, as the candles in their glass holders went out one by one. Gérard wondered if they felt, as she did, those fleeting waves pass over her brain, the excitement and the joy of every cell in her body being brought to life, heated, the panic of feeling that it was finally happening, the cocoon was rupturing in a secret explosion of the universe, a universe that could do nothing but explode every second in every way, thought Gérard, the planet was devouring itself with its pits of fire, its masked or gigantic wars, a little bit everywhere, and soon we wouldn't even have enough water to live, the earth had been burned so much, leaving nothing among the ashes of sterile fields but spirits of men, women, and children decimated by the other war, famine. What was Gérard, with her private nervous, euphoric explosion, amidst that massive conflagration from which there would remain nothing but debris? A green garden, a secluded lake, beautiful mementos of childhood, and all around, ashes as far as the eye could see, on those sterile fields that the spirits of the dead floated over, or living skeletons that would soon be cadavers, faces emaciated in the sun, glassy stare fixed in place below their eyelids, surrounded by the buzz of flies against the white, empty sky, thought Gérard, wondering if that was the reason she was so hostile by the light of day, that light which, be it cold or hot, bore witness to all disaster. She had not seen the spring, much less the summer with its intense light that pierced the flesh at midday — she begged Doudouline and Polydor to let her close the curtains until the evening — but in the summer the nosy light crept its way everywhere, over the sheets and the unmade beds: curled up in that indecent stream of light that was often dirty in the cities. Gérard was astonished that anyone could live in that daytime air where all was transparent and ugly, where faces took on livid tints in the street. That united couple, Doudouline and Polydor, was always there, but after Johnie's flight, and the thought of all those adventures she could be having far away, Gérard did not like couples that summer, the fusion of their skin bothered her almost as much as the sun, Doudouline and Polydor went outside together, at Sophie's house, they went swimming together in her lake, they went sailing together in Sophie's boat, and this constant doubleness in everything — love, sports, love, how it annoyed Gérard to see all around her that doubled, screaming vitality when she herself had so little — absorbed all of Gérard's energy, and, neglected, she wasted away in Abeille's apartment. When she got up at the end of the day, she was surrounded by cigarettes crushed out in ashtrays and the blond bitterness of beer at the bottom of bottles and glasses — no one washed the dishes anymore since Thérèse had left, let alone the clothes that they stuffed into black bags in the hallway until Polydor began to shout and Doudouline calmed her saying in her melodic voice "What a reaction, God, what a reaction, for something so trivial, we'll do the laundry one of these days." — in Abeille's living room that had once been so clean in the days Thérèse was reigning there, with her jogging shoes or her skis, Thérèse incarnate and present, not just her phantom in a painting, even if she had been kind enough to smile while she was being painted. A real person had deserted while looking at that painting in Abeille's living room, before that silence where Gérard was thinking about the white, empty sky of the Sudan and those pale phantoms that had died of hunger and were still wandering over the ashes, and that was it, Gérard could hear the roar of the silence, a roar that came from the walls, from the bedrooms they had left in haste, two by two, underwear and stockings were still tangled up under the beds, and those objects always appeared, in twos, in their intertwinings, the fusion of the twisted vines of their wool or cotton underthings. It wasn't like the time when you would hear the sound of Johnie's pen scratching on the paper, even if Gérard hated that writing — writing and its obstacles, the solitude, the discipline, the sanity that it required of Johnie — for Johnie barely had to lean toward her pages, her notebooks, for the writer in her to become dark, metamorphose into a taciturn, morose being, thought Gérard. What could there be there that was so sorrowfully inaccessible? It was the hour that, in the shadowy light, Gérard heard voices and saw incongruous forms on the walls and in the folds of the curtains, the hour of trembling and fear, she thought, like the hour of need — and meanwhile Doudouline and Polydor were disrupting Sophie's peaceful countryside with their cargo of tents and sleeping bags — Sophie made sure they did not invade her chalet, they would mess up everything, she said, her silver spoons and forks, even her beauty creams that they used up, and her shouting could be heard to the depths of the forest when she was mad at the girls, Gérard thought. Doudouline walked ahead with her voluptuous curves — and what a pity, thought Polydor, that Doudouline was becoming visibly thinner — undulating underneath her silk tunic, still complaining about the steepness of the hills and mountains. Polydor climbed the slopes and paths behind her, for Doudouline, a queen that would carry nothing but herself, had entrusted her with all the provisions, and sweat ran down Polydor's pointed face, below the mass of her hair, the black lines of her eyebrows, as she wondered why Saint John of the Cross had loved Jesus Christ so much, Christ was not a serene man because he had to suffer so for the salvation of men. It was possible to love only in serenity, otherwise you got lost like Saint John of the Cross. How was it that Doudouline took such delight, in her dreams at night, in the grass, in the moss of the woods, while here, in this forest, far away from her arid nighttime spirituality, she let out screams if a thorn grazed her rosy, tender foot? That foot that Polydor couldn't kiss or squeeze rather tightly in her hand — that thought brought her back to Saint John of the Cross and his sensuality linked to the torment of Christ's face — without hearing the soft wailing that came from Doudouline whose trembling skin was so easily damaged, like her tunics and nightgowns, and that depraved Abeille who had run off to Mexico with Paula and could have been climbing the Mayan temples of the Yucatan sitting on Paula's shoulders, letting her legs hang down on Paula's breasts, she seemed minuscule so far away, like those children that brought tourists on a slow ascension that looked like an offering of fragility to the gods of the stone: Abeille was going to leave Paula when she got back, she had written in a postcard to Polydor. What a trip to hell, a fanatic who beat her, thought Polydor. Abeille would have done better to pursue her voyage in her bedroom, head on her pillow, watching the swarm of cracks in the ceiling, who could know when she would come back now? Like Johnie, who was left immobile on a dock by a trip to the ocean and could barely move, sunk into an uncomfortable chair at an open bar beneath the sky with its tables and chairs and its impressive décor that floated towards eternity, Johnie had stopped before the sky and alone turned up the collar of her raincoat in the hot air that was swelling with storms while the red and white end of her cigarette glowed at her fingertips. A luxurious ocean liner swayed on the green water for a time before cutting the waves of the open sea; its iridescent lettering sparkled like the sun on the sea, it was the *Grand Mudder*, which for a fabulous sum, was carrying its cargo all the way to New Orleans, and a few men and women of some royal lineage were waiting on the dock with a mournful air in their polished shoes and their grey flannel pants below aquamarine vests with gilded buttons, the image of feigned naïveté that transformed them into eternal university monarchs who never would have studied, they seemed to have been born into a life of luxury drifting along in complete vacuity, but a splendid vacuity. Like Johnie who did nothing herself, she thought, but would not be rolling over the waves in that boat tonight, enjoying its roomy cabins in that city where time stood still, in which each person had a private theater and chapel and the calm of a suddenly monstrous sea that could have swallowed up in its depths all that gold and the pomp of such vanity. Standing right near the rigging, as the sailors in white shorts energetically washed the panels of the ship's hold, were three junkies dressed in rags with faces that trembled in the air like three brown spots, and the indiscretion of their presence could be quickly pointed out so they could be chased away — which the captain, who saw them, did not do, but condescendingly looked the three boys and the brown spots of their faces up and down — standing paralyzed among the rigging, they balanced with solemnity above the water. A teenaged boy with his hair drawn up on his head like a bundle of hay who was luring the pelicans with bits of fish from his modest fishing boat — they came to perch on his shoulder, knocking their carnivores' wings against his cheek — shouted gleeful insults at the mates on the liner who were his friends. "Hey, Grand Mudder, Mother Fucker, when you gonna come tuna fishing for five bucks a day?" Probably out of respect for the captain who was still standing outside of his cabin, the sailors did not respond except with a smile to the tauntings of the boy who was bending, below the pelicans, toward the bottom of his boat where there was too much water and snorting with laughter, with the same smile that lit up the faces of the young people at their menial work on the ocean liner. Johnie, however, had felt the melancholy of evil express itself, and again she thought of the imperative hand of God or some other unknown divinity that must have nailed her down there, in her wooden chair with all of them, the three junkies standing in the rigging, the fisherman underneath the pelicans, she too was a victim of the soft suffocation of the day, she had lost all her spirit like when she had put her hand on Marianne's back during those hours of meditation when nothing happened, except waiting for the acute, supreme well-being, the purpose of love, that she would soon be submerged in. And suddenly, when Marianne's arms closed around her, Johnie thought of Gérard, whom she had so often showered with tenderness in bed — showered because Gérard got up again immediately to take her medications, she had to take some every hour in the bathroom — and Thérèse wasn't there to throw them systematically into the toilet, and Thérèse's words suddenly seemed so harsh: "Ah! Girls, I'm sick of always having to make your decisions for you. I'm leaving, maybe you'll take better care of yourselves without me!" Gérard, if she decided to disappear, would leave no more trace than those sea snakes in the Philippines and Peru whose lives were spent in the black of the sea, underneath emerald and coral reefs, after their mating ceremonies, in a light they couldn't bear. Like those snakes hunted by predators for their fine skin, Gérard could also sense the hunter's arrow, the threat of her rapid extinction she had so often spoken of to Johnie, the end of a universe that would be linked to her own end, in the ashes of one selfsame agony, Gérard and the world. And Marianne's back was there, in the closed bedroom, and her discussions of Schopenhauer when she didn't know how to get rid of boredom — did Johnie want to come read next to her, was it too hot or too cold, was there going to be a storm? — and reading Schopenhauer was not reassuring to Johnie as she covered Marianne's back with the pressure of her widely spread fingers, and yesterday, Gérard's back, the projection of bones under the straight shoulders Johnie had felt beneath her fingers when the being that was Gérard, the complexity of her nature that she deviated from so minimally, repeating that there was nothing serious in existence, that entire being revealed to her by the placidity of her body, when you contemplated her, a network of pale veins that ran beneath her skin which suddenly seemed to solidify like marble in the sleep and the laziness of love. But Gérard hadn't written to her, and in the stretch of vain hours at the end of a dock Johnie thought that eternity was already upon the earth — even that funereal destruction of the earth that Gérard feared which seemed to bring itself about slowly, by erosion —

while she was trapped between the sky and the ocean, an eternity in which she was deprived of Lynda and almost deafened by the impending racket of the *Grand Mudder* on a sea that was suddenly obscured by the approaching winds, when the liner split itself away from the port to whip at the waves as it belched its crown of smoke from under the flags at the sky; wouldn't she too feel that same pain of separation from the earth, like the three boys with brown faces hanging slackly on to the nets of the rigging and the carefree tuna fisherman pirouetting in his water-filled boat. There would be imperceptible shocks under the earth that would reach Johnie's heart, like when she was near Marianne, a few days more on a pile of pebbles, a sort of sinister beach that had been craftily put together for military plans but given up to vacationers, with its pebbled walkways and granite dunes, the center of an implacably blue sea, sitting on the pedestal of the war, for people bathed and swam in that sea that was shot through with deathly radiation, that beach that no trees encircled, where you could barely distinguish a man or woman who, testing the depth of the water, was descending to an immense funeral pyre, and Johnie had thought that the sky had been blocked by the ocean at the hand of man on that beach heavy with his machines of death, which, though they were no longer installed there, haunted the forbidding bareness of the countryside and the silence of that ocean devoid of contours and deserted by fauna. Sitting on her foam mattress, Marianne was typing a letter on that beach, writing to her secretary in New York, worried about a painting that was being sold, a museum that was opening in Jerusalem although the ocean, the sea, was no more than a center, only that: a huge eye that spied on them, like the eye of a cannon. Marianne grew irritated also at Johnie's questions about her life — did she love her husband, her lovers, what was she doing with Johnie if she had such a full life? And to that Marianne responded dryly that a man and a woman, except for the sexual energy that brought them together, were two strangers to each other and the she owed Johnie no further explanation — and it was at that moment, as she listened to the clacking of the electronic typewriter under Marianne's fingers that handled that object briskly, that Johnie had thought of the agony of those sea snakes in the Philippines and Peru and Gérard, whose soft, flexible coils, like those of the snakes as they slept, had not been stretched out in the light of day, for the day represented for Gérard the absurdity of that murderous or soon to be murderous beach, the pain of deluded, slaughtered nature without the song of the birds, except for the jingle of future weapons that you heard in the air already, even if happy black natives were playing tambourines and singing far away, they said, knowing nothing of their destiny. And despite this, sitting on that beach that was entrenched below, already sprinkled with blood under the pebbles and fine sand, Marianne was typing a letter with as much determination, strength, and courage as the *Grand Mudder* on the water that was fading away, soon to be released into the tempest. "I've done a lot of work for this museum in Jerusalem" she was saying in her soft foreign voice, indifferent to the disturbance of places that worried Johnie, as if Marianne had been looking at the strangeness of the sky and that beach with an expression of conquering complicity below her wide-brimmed hat: or wasn't it more of an expression of triumph, the sign of a will for endurance and determination as if Marianne had decided that life would go on normally for her on that island, despite the fatal detonations in the Pacific? And, that moment of terror having passed, in the face of Marianne's tenacity, the continuation of her business on a deserted beach, amid the commotion of electronic notes, the *Grand Mudder* breached the waves and the sky, disappearing with its phantom passengers who were still waving on the bridge, and Johnie felt that her eternity was drifting with all of them and with the three brown-faced boys who had fallen from the heights of the rigging with their dreams and were now looking at the tips of their feet through their holey socks. Then came that trio from Berlin who had been late leaving, standing on the gangway, a man, a woman, and their daughter, a family Johnie had often noticed perched on the terraces with the island birds, they had landed here in a whirlwind of noisy parties, everywhere Johnie had noticed a sort of dullness in the joy on their chubby faces: in the sun, on their balcony overlooking the sea, like in the middle of the night as they continued their feasts, gorging themselves before the eyes of the servants who waited patiently for this gluttony to be over so they could go to sleep. Everywhere, she had heard their laughing, if they were half-naked, darker than the natives under their blond body hair or decked out in their pink and white cotton clothes, the young girl discovering her pubescent breasts on the beach or the father offering his round penis under the transparent nylon of his bikini bathing suit, they were enjoying themselves more than anyone else, as if for themselves alone, thought Johnie in this suspicious era we live in. Inseparable and identical with their thick blond curls that they shook in the wind, they bathed in the innocence of prosperity, having barely come out alive from the craters of History where their parents had buried so much wreckage. That was the miracle, that they were glowing with health as they emerged from ruins. And suddenly, before rejoining the travelers on the liner, they had hesitated an instant, huddling together on the gangway, under the velocity of the wind and the black clouds that were gathering above their heads. They were no more than three hands waving together on the bridge, and the *Grand Mudder* was disappearing into a warm fog with its soon to be invisible passengers and the lifeboats roped to its sides, like those temporary rafts, tiny as canoes, that you saw on the sides of tall warships.

§

And Paula slowly dragged herself up to the top of the temple, spread her long legs, one foot pointing to the north, the other to the south, like when she was walking down the street, where she had more than once fallen and broken a leg. She would soon be at the uppermost point of the pyramid, thought Abeille looking at that pale, soldier-like figure under the sun that was heating her to white-hot, thinking "I can't go on, she's so strong, she'll be the death of me yet." And Paula, her arms crossed, fixed her piercing eye on Abeille, a graceful flower in the razed, arid countryside that she was now scanning with her eagle eye. Who were all these girls of no character that praised her, with their whims and their fears, if she dared to correct them with a slightly firm slap or a pinch on the calf, yes, who were they? Little children of no importance, puppies abandoned on the doorstep in winter, and you let them come in and get warm in your house. A slap hurts nothing but one's pride — hadn't the paternal lesson been more rigid when Paula had twice tried to drown her sisters? Recipe for getting rid of your sisters when you are your mother's son, Paula had written in her slow, sure precocity, and, said Madame Boudreau, the doctor had suffered greatly reading the jealous message his daughter had written, suffered so much that he had made her buttocks permanently red with his belt, which was difficult because Paula had hidden under her mother's bed and, as the doctor's wife didn't want to do it, he had had to resort to pulling her out by her spidery legs. First you go on vacation with your mother and father, wrote Paula, and you're good in the hotel in the evenings, don't talk to adults during meals and don't move in your chair. When the next day comes you go out to the dock, in Rimouski there's a lot of water, take an empty box of apples and fill it up, when your two sisters are inside, close the box, tie it shut with a rope, leave two holes for breathing, then there's nothing left to do but throw the box into the water. And she listened to barbarous songs in English, no pride in her own language, no patriotic or nationalist attachments, nothing, while the last Français d'Amérique, like the whales and falcons, were threatened with extinction — but for Abeille, that country Paula talked about was a free, insane paradise where the great poets had struck themselves down in the college courtyards, where the blood was still running over the snow, it must be truly evil, this country that had permitted such breakage of spirit and conscience, this country whose blood and genius artists' deaths the incurable glory of Abeille's elders, like Paula, fed off of? Paula was breathing hard, taken over by the grandeur of the Toltec warriors among their hatchets and their palm trees sculpted in the rough stone, seeking with their busy fingers the form of a fire serpent that had long been the symbol of the powers of day and night and now, forever subjugated, slept in the dust of a monument. (She was also looking for her pack of cigarettes that she'd forgotten among Abeille's things and swearing with rage.) She was digging with her fingers through the pocket of her beige shorts, beneath the big red striped blouse with its tails coming out of the leather belt of her shorts, no cigarettes, nothing, and that girl down there who was looking at her she would eventually have under control, she too, like the others. They were men's shorts, thought Abeille, with women's panties underneath that were so worn that they were no more than lace swaddling that Paula was bursting out of victorious, quick with her hands, the area was deserted, Abeille could have fled. Paula was taming the black spiders, the tarantulas, she would certainly bring all her friends to Mexico, there was that appalling discharge of the bowels into the metal buckets that took the place of sanitary toilets in the sordid restaurants, thought Abeille, the jungle was so close behind as Paula sang her praises for Mayan culture and those balls of venom in all the rooms under the folds of the shower curtains, like in a swimming pool when you let the water out. And she has no education and doesn't want to learn anything, thought Paula up on the wall, dreaming about that tribe that had been called the People of the Sun, defeated, vaporized, enslaved, our virile tribe that could have become an honorable civilization, Paula also thought, turning her proud profile towards the sky whitened like lime beneath the harshness of the light, to live, what a degrading misery sometimes, especially without alcohol, without cigarettes, talk to them about the polytheist religion of the Aztecs and you'll see what ignorance they live in! Paula again saw the serpent that had coiled massively on the table during dinner the night before, it had seized them while she was explaining to Abeille — didn't she have to explain everything to them? — that Tlaloc was the god of rain and Quetzalcoatl was the god of air and water, Tlaloc, Quetzalcoatl, and suddenly there it was in the middle of the salad: "A boa!" Abeille had shouted. It was a reptile of modest size, stunned by the fall from the tree. A boy who was sauntering around with his pitcher of water had promptly given it quite an adroit blow with a stick, just one, Abeille had thought, looking at Paula, erect and petrified with terror on her straw chair, like at the hotel on vacation with her parents and Madame Boudreau, one never got up from the table before the end of the meal, and she would wait, even if her cheeks were stuffed with lumps of bread that she hadn't had time to chew in the shock of snakes, iguanas — that afternoon she had thought she felt an iguana under her foot — Tlaloc, god of the rain, Quetzalcoatl. Perhaps she had been too severe with Abeille that morning, she would pay better attention in the future. Abeille seemed to be holding back tears behind her glasses that were fogged with sweat; that girl would have saved her, after all, she had run along those iguanas lying flat against the hot stones to that lost beach where it was forbidden to bathe, but Paula would go anyway, she never did what other people did, who was there to stop her from going to the site of bewitching death on a beach at the end of the world, and Abeille had soon heard Paula's long scream that split the white sky from between the cliffs and had run until her feet bled, in the brambles, waking up a German man who was asleep in his hut, the only explorer on that virgin beach, whose sailboat was resting half-buried in the sand among the remains of fish, when she heard that scream that pierced the air, Paula saying, "I'm drowning, I' m drowning." The man had bounded into the waves with heroic courage, and the echo of his voice could be heard: "Ich komme, ich komme," while Abeille swam backstroke into the boiling waves, the man's light chestnut hair shone in the reflections of the water; Abeille could see nothing of Paula but her strong fist stretched up towards the livid sky, and it was towards that fist — that hand that struck women, but so lightly, Paula would have said, for like wolves and huge dogs, Paula, who knows, Abeille thought, didn't know her own strength — towards Paula's wild hand that Abeille and the brave man had clung to to drag Paula back to the shore where she had vomited all the water of the ocean as the man roughly slapped her cheeks which were white and blue and suddenly so hollow beneath her sparse hair, wet with foam and algae. But once relieved of that catastrophe that had hampered her for an instant, Paula went back down the steps of the temple, Abeille brandishing her pack of cigarettes from afar. She wanted nothing else from her then, Paula had nearly been rescued by a stranger, in fact, she had been — someone who didn't speak her language, she reflected, shocked — and she felt an urgent need to smoke, to grab Abeille who was squatting on a mound of grass — still a turista, this generation has no immunity, not like us, this is my twelfth trip to Mexico and I'm never sick — to kiss her, take her in her arms as she was feeling the arousal of love again after her brush with death. Wasn't love the only permissible sensation in life, she thought, and she prudently placed her feet one after the other on the stone steps, and then Abeille had held her pack of cigarettes out to her without a word. That silence had astounded Paula who was afraid, her pale face turned toward the sun.

§

Coming back to the moist heat of the big cities in summer, far from the English isle and from Marianne, who was now in Jerusalem where she would be opening a museum, Johnie again felt herself pierced by an arrow of imprecise pain, Gérard was there, not seeing her in the shadows on the dance floor at that hour of dawn when the Club was deserted, Gérard was alone, sniffing her white powder as her face relaxed little by little in the agitation of a pleasure, as mysterious and guilty as when she offered her lips to a stranger, a pleasure at once fearful and frantic, thought Johnie, that suddenly isolated Gérard and her milieu, the milieu of the Club with its blue light and candles in glasses, in a clandestine but proud well-being that reminded Johnie of the extent to which destiny, even when it raises us at times above ourselves, sets us apart, at the moment when we expect the least from it, from those abject surprises, as she was living now watching Gérard. She thought about that story Marianne had told her: The Masais, to feed on the milk and blood of their cattle, would puncture the animal's jugular vein with an arrow with a rounded tip and then collect the blood in a gourd. Not approving of these sacrifices, but at the mercy of harsh necessities like the weak-legged goats and cows that scraped at infertile soil, it now seemed to Johnie that Gérard had decided to perish this way, or perhaps it was Johnie who was losing blood little by little as her own veins were punctured with an arrow with a rounded tip. That too had to be the will of God, that crazy divinity that

Johnie did not love but that urged her anyway to read the Book of Revelations with an increasingly tormented conscience, whether she was alone, listening to a Bach mass, her headphones on her ears, or hanging around Marianne in a bedroom where the last rays of sun on a crumpled sheet were making her lose her mind. God, she was certain, when he began to speak to creatures in a language as sonorous as it was violent, could only render them insane, and it was God also that afflicted Gérard with lightning and curses. Johnie felt all her inability to draw to her that drifting face that no longer spoke to her — though Abeille would not have taken time to reflect, she would have seized Gérard by the straps of her overalls and given her a vigorous spank — Gérard's face that Johnie had known only in the intimacy of those illuminating moments when, a short time ago, a cheek sunk into a pillow below a tuft of hair, the gleam of teeth in a smile, or the persistence of an amused look in the morning when Gérard didn't know whether she was going to sleep or getting up, had held for Johnie their own surprise, their own light. She got up, standing still at the end of the dock in the glare of the sun or under the thick clouds that had carried the *Grand Mudder* to the horizon. She had abandoned Gérard to her fate cold-heartedly, she thought, loving Marianne while Gérard was floating alone towards deadly territory, Gérard had not come out of the winter while Doudouline and Polydor were tanning in the sun. "Come home with me," said Johnie, and these words had barely been pronounced, in one breath, "home with me," when Johnie saw the many signs of her suffering light up, the razor left by the man who had invaded a space that had been so secret, Gérard's cap that symbolized the subtlety of lying and transgression, and on a chest in the bedroom, the heap of multi-colored envelopes that contained Lynda's letters, the words Lynda had written, the juicy letters that filled all the pages, and Johnie dreaded their calm incandescence, their ultimate cruelty, for in them Lynda would talk about her life, her travels in Europe and Africa, with him, the man, the invader whose face Johnie in her disgust never even imagined. "Home," said Johnie, and she had dragged Gérard, her body stiff and far away in its isolation, even if Gérard had had many one-night-stands since she'd been selling drugs, by the hand to her apartment on the second floor, who as soon as Johnie had opened the door, without even looking at her, had thrown herself on the bed fully dressed with such an alarming laugh that Johnie had thought the world was collapsing and under Gérard's eyelashes — she was sleeping now, barely breathing — and on her forehead and her pallid cheeks, sorrow was beginning to settle: Johnie saw before her again a woman who was often seen on the streets of the neighborhood, alone, talking to herself, crossing the street between cars carrying her two-year-old son on her shoulders. The child sitting on his mother's shoulders, hands clasped around a forehead that was his only treasure on the earth, that child determined to live despite such hardship, with no spark of understanding or reason to guide him, and the woman who carried him on her shoulders shaking him left and right like a package with no strings, weren't these two, thought Johnie, the victims of a decay bred by a *fin de siècle* that was already burying its living? Johnie had placed her hand on Gérard's head, that heavy head that eluded her even in sleep; she remembered the smell of hash that penetrated all of Lynda's clothes, whether she was with Johnie in the country brushing shoulders with barbarity, with her wiggly walk defying the police guards or the customs officials who felt nothing but disdain for white women, or in a prison in Turkey where she had languished, never afraid, for more than a week, or in the disarray of her bedroom next to Johnie. You could smell it on her neck, often mixed with her perfume, the burned odor of hash and see the glow of her joint at her lips at night along with that dreamlike mist that sometimes extended the pleasure of love. Hash had always been part of Lynda's life, as it had been part of Gérard's life, thought Johnie. And if Gérard was taking narcotics stronger than hash, if the corrupting needle had already shocked her brain, wouldn't she go out like the fires that those lost hunters lit in the forest during winter nights? But hadn't Lynda survived it all, Johnie thought also, the juvenile reform school at thirteen, she said, a rape in a train by four soldiers, her prison cell in Turkey where she could even stretch out in the sun, in court while policemen and cocaine dealers held discussions among themselves? And suddenly, in Turkey or somewhere else, Johnie had seen Lynda spring up in front of her, in those train stations that looked like stone caverns where Johnie had morbidly felt her exile as if she had been imprisoned in the brownish stone of the stations with that sea of faces that she protected, faces in which Johnie distinguished only the crack of the mouth, and beneath the hoods of bomber jackets that covered their foreheads, the tumescence of an eye fixed upon her, bloodshot, as if the wounds of misery and hunger had begun to desiccate in the sun, under the wide, hazy eyelids of those strangers who came from everywhere in their mute exodus, getting off a steamer with their humble trunks and later jostling each other in the stations, in the cities where they landed as orphans already scorned by all, as the light burned the rails, carved up the countryside with its rays of fire among the pink houses with their flat roofs and withered vines. And Lynda shook the warm halo of her crystal laugh, she ran toward Johnie, holding lemons and oranges that she had gathered in the market against her chest. In the air, along with the fragrance of orange and lemon trees that Lynda brought back from their dark regions, was the aroma of grilled meat that was sold on the street in the intense heat, and in Lynda's hair — she was panting from having run — was that compelling smell of hash that evoked in Johnie such distressing sensations of ennui and torpor, like she was feeling now as she looked at Gérard.

No sudden noises, Johnie thought, not even the trembling of the leaves in the trees, weighed down by the hot air of the street, silence reigned alone in the apartment that was already so quiet in the summer, with Gérard's irregular breathing that you could barely hear, as Gérard was someplace else, someplace where she wasn't suffering and only through the narrow slit of her eyelids noticed Johnie pacing nervously through the apartment as if she were on the verge of calling for help or sometimes coming to sit down on the bed next to Gérard, who she was watching with a painful feeling of helplessness as Gérard was reeling in a white, liquid zone — perhaps she had fainted, collapsing against the wall of the Club like the last time — where bad dreams became as tangible as reality; you would have thought it was there between her fingers again, the rabbit she had accidentally strangled one Easter day, the chicks in a box were there too, with their new feathers that no one dared to touch, killed by Gérard's exuberance, amusement, joy that gave way before the abundance of gifts that her adoptive parents offered to her.

How was it that she had squeezed its neck too hard, that mass of fur and its blood that was spilling onto the rug, how had this massacre come about, this tragedy in the living room, perhaps it was fear that had killed it, she had only to close her fingers, those magnanimous parents who had adopted a little girl, who were they, quickly going grey, going to Florida in the winter, cultivating their garden in the summer, down on their knees in the earth, their foreheads and cheeks wrinkled already, though Gérard would have liked never to lose them, never to leave them. They themselves said, "When we're not here anymore, you will be alone in the world," and that mound of ashes was there on the horizon, under which the rabbit had been buried. And what day was it that Gérard had tried on her dinner jacket, standing on the kitchen table while her mother fixed the hem of her pants? It was then that Gérard had thought of the rabbit incident, putting her hand on her mother's head as she sewed. Who were they, who were they, why had they chosen her — and the dinner jacket had a red silk lining. It was for going out to the Club at night, they knew, it's important for young people to have fun, they said in their gentle senility. If Gérard thought often about the ashes, it was because she knew that one day they would be cremated, and she repeated this word to herself as she put her hand on the grey head of her mother: Mother will be cremated, there are fires everywhere, not one place where they don't burn. They had unfolded a newspaper onto the table where she was standing, her outfit was still lacking a sleeve, but in that paper could be seen fire and blood mixed together and skeletal shadows on the charred fields in the Sudan, fire and blood mixing together before the eyes of the old lady who was hemming a pant leg for her daughter, vicious battles were going on, but she knew nothing about them, they would be going to Florida for the winter, fleeing the cold and the blood that ran elsewhere or coagulated like it had from the murdered rabbit, the rabbit Gérard had been given at Easter along with the chicks in their box, and later on, Gérard would be going to the Club in her dinner jacket with the red silk lining.

§

And Sophie thought that in that dense heat they couldn't have their lunch outside, there were already too many flies on the terrace. But before eight in the morning she had already done her exercises, made an omelet and coffee for the girls who, since the night before, had been invading her countryside with their tents and sleeping bags — but it was better to see them out there among the fir trees than here in her chalet with their feet still muddy with water from the lake. She had even memorized her lines for the evening rehearsal (it was a good hour to the city even if she drove fast), it was inexplicable how she had been feeling so invaded since Doudouline had been there, playing with her sailboat, bathing in her lake with Polydor, a mother did not have the right to feel that within herself, it was an injustice, an anomaly, but when the girls were there, her countryside was slightly altered, even when she was watering her flower garden she felt spied upon. Doudouline was well aware that Sophie hid her silver when they came, in the antique chest of drawers she had the key to. Sophie had never possessed anything before, and suddenly her countryside was easily hurt, the leaves on the trees were shaking in a bad way. Where were the order and peace she needed so much? Those girls affected her silence, she was already having trouble concentrating, wondering if perhaps she had never understood that Strindberg play she'd acted in so often, was it because of lack of concentration or because she was nothing but an instinctive creature of the stage, self-taught and deprived of basic knowledge? Now she was advancing towards her countryside with great strides, yes, it was an unease that she preferred not to explain to herself. Polydor was walking ahead with the knapsacks, Doudouline was coming up behind, chasing away a wasp with her hand. From the terrace Sophie saw the mountain where people skied in the winter, the lake calm below. A man, far off, who had gotten up at the same time as Sophie, was swimming alone, lifting mechanical arms towards the sun, he too dedicated himself to exercise in the morning, as Sophie had done taking long breaths with each movement. If Sophie earned a lot of money on television, in the theater, and during the summer theater season, she didn't do it to waste it, squander it all, though before, at the commune, it was fine if they had enough money for heat. Washing sheets at the pump, how horrible! Now she had her sauna, her pool and here in the country a mountain, a lake, but who was still thinking about the hardships of the past? Her son was a hoodlum who had robbed his father on the day of their divorce, running off with his two leather suitcases. Doudouline would be an expensive liability with her group of rock musicians but it was a good investment for her future career. If only she could have gotten married like everyone else, that exists also, men, Sophie had had quite a few of her own, she had even known passion. For Doudouline, Polydor, the concern was mood and taste, certainly, they had already discussed it among themselves, but even so, Polydor, with her theology, the priesthood for a woman, like homosexuality, was not a future. It was an amusing generation, you could tell they hadn't witnessed World War II; they were over privileged. Abeille, for example, with her paintings, Gérard, who had such a flair for comedy — though she had never given her that Molière part, no, she had hesitated, there were so many out-of-work comedians, after all — and could imitate all the commercials on television, what was it they all found so pleasant about living with one another? It was frustrating sometimes, some men understood, others didn't, it is truly complicated for them to imagine what goes on inside the hearts of women. Doudouline, Polydor were drawing closer and closer, thrusting aside a branch that whipped the hot, heavy air. They wouldn't eat outside today, thought Sophie, fortunately she had had time to do work for her playwright before the girls had arrived, already she could hear them laughing, squabbling under the trees; "Come on, come on," shouted Sophie, suddenly delighted to see them, she felt rejuvenated — this wouldn't last, she thought, the old annoyances would quickly return — by their presence. "The coffee's ready, so is the toast." She smiles with her pretty mouth contracted, thought Doudouline, dear mother, she never changes. And for Doudouline the climb had been long and painful, that diet was going to kill her, she thought as she looked at her mother on the terrace who had locked the silver in the antique chest. "Oh, mother, after that night under the beautiful stars we're dying of hunger," Doudouline had said in her singing voice, and despite the flies and the heat, in the first buzzings of the day, they had had lunch together on the terrace and Doudouline had eaten so much that she had suddenly fallen into giddy immobility, unbuttoning her jeans under her Indian tunic while her mother was looking off to the distance, towards her mountain and her lake. And Gérard? They hadn't brought Gérard, Doudouline had thought suddenly, where was Gérard, with her pills that she took from morning till evening, and even during the night, for the liver, the heart, tingling skin, though she was in perfectly good health. What would you do with a hypochondriac out in the fields? She was afraid of water and, what was more, became extremely melancholy when she saw a lake. They didn't know where Gérard was these days, the sun's rays no longer shone through the blinds in her bedroom, it was agonizing, thought Doudouline, there was no one left at the house except that couple, Doudouline and Polydor, the place was so bare when stripped of its fruit — Polydor, never losing hope, continued to prepare meals for the others every day, continued to feed the cat, and she wasn't mistaken, thought Doudouline, because someone always ended up coming by, Abeille come to complain about Paula, Paula the irascible, the moody, that she was never without. That couple was so fragile before Sophie who was looking at the scenery with satisfaction, for she was finally well-rooted there, after her whole life as an exile in Paris, thought Doudouline, and she's an elegant mother who doesn't wear T-shirts with sweat stains under the arms like Polydor, whose hair had been curled at the hairdresser's the day before, and would waste no time in asking "So finally, girls, do you have a goal in life? You're planning studies — no work, no money. How long do you intend to keep living this way?" But Sophie said nothing, made a barely perceptible gesture of irritation, carelessly shaking her beautiful head of red hair as Doudouline told her with a professional air that she was still looking for a bass and a guitar for her show: "See, you always count on me to find them, and the lighting, the technical production, have you thought about that, too?" And Doudouline thought that the white fluffy cloud was threatening to become a storm cloud in the sky. How could an artist mother and daughter, this couple of an excessive individualism, coexist? But no, the thick cloud was dissolving in the burning sky, grazing the pines and fir trees, Sophie was positive, despite everything, she thought, that Strindberg had not understood women — she hadn't been to drama school like so many others, nor yet the Beaux Arts in Paris, like Paula, the proletarian, she would be there till the day she died, no one ever raised themselves up from their condition, all that was dreams, lies — and this reminded her of an argument she'd had with Paula on the subject of Strindberg, Ibsen. Strindberg had described the greed, the spitefulness of women without knowing what caused it, he had never lived in the abjection of their daily lives, she admired him only for his passionate socialism. The living playwrights here played tennis, never left their circle — often comfortable chauvinists, they held no threat for her because she had already had one as a husband. The playwright she was studying now was an exception, seemed to her to go too far, with his scenes of prostitution and drugs, she would go to the East to see what that was like. Sophie believed only in the truth, she thought. Paula, whose father hadn't been a plumber, could easily say that Strindberg was the analyst of the female subconscious, nothing proved that that was true, he had never been torn between profession and family as Sophie was. And now Polydor was knitting her brows and saying to Doudouline as she put her hand on her knee, "We should have brought Gérard — where *could* she be?" It was so hot that a mist was falling over the lake, it would soon be time to go swimming, and those two sweat stains under the arms of Polydor's T-shirt were still there, Doudouline noticed, as she threw a quick glance at her mother who seemed to be lost in her thoughts, a faraway look on her face below her red hair.

§

The construction of the roof had been a great source of worry to Thérèse. With the help of her apprentices — her delinquent apprentices who had come from a home where Thérèse worked with other psychologists and social workers — the work on the roof was finished now, those sleepless nights of thinking about the roof, the gutter-pipe, the windows, the chimney, not to mention the bedrooms in the basement for the girls, and Abeille's studio that let in all the sun at noon, the narrow boundaries of the yard (where would Thérèse park her car, where would her main entry and staircase be?), those days among the construction materials that were still lying around on the denuded patch of lawn next to the door, the garden would be left for another year, everywhere piles of wood, brick, concrete, and what could she do about those homeless people who came to consult her round the clock while she was fretting about the masses of her files, her class notes, all this despite the miracle of her computer, a portable that gave her difficult gifts: all of these vagrants had the strong desire to better their lot, but how could they with their monthly check, comparable to the salary of an Ethiopian, though we were not in Ethiopia — ah! that diaphanous disorder in Abeille's living room at dawn, when Gérard was smoking her last joint, in the sun's rays that were so pale in winter, under that roof that leaned a bit too much to the left, the error of the apprentice — Thérèse was pacing up and down, because even though she had gotten up at six, she hadn't had time to go to the mountain today, wondering if the Minister of Health understood his responsibilities with his stingy budget for the underprivileged, it was inscribed into her computer, that .0114352 percent of the budget allotted to the Ethiopians of our streets, our cities. Thérèse's health, also, was declining a bit, even if she took all those mineral-based products proclaimed to have qualities to revitalize the organism, like chamomile, which cured the headaches she often had, lucerne, a tonic for the stomach, thyme, a powerful detoxifier, though she was too young to suffer the insidious pains of arthritis and gout, licorice root, which the Greeks and Romans had used to heal the grippe and bronchitis, but Thérèse ran every day along the river, which was contaminated by all the waste from the surrounding factories, and had never had a cold, running each morning in her blue striped shorts and the white socks and running shoes that went with them on the banks, she aired out her lungs in a vapor of microbes that were killed by all those minerals, the highly praised calcium, iodine, iron, magnesium, and potassium she took when she got up, in the form of pills, each one, like the invention of molecular biology, a promise of eternity in a world that was self-destructing at its base. But if the plants provided us with this ephemeral survival, especially if we didn't drink, didn't pollute the atmosphere, the abominable zero percent targeted to the homeless that always showed up on the screen of her computer tormented Thérèse day and night, so completely that she forgot the existence of Abeille and the hot body she had held in her arms for so many nights. Yes, thought Thérèse, throughout all those glacial winter nights Jean had slept in the entry hall of a building before he was kicked and chased out onto the street, Gisèle, who came from Bas-du-Fleuve, had slept in the subway and been likewise rejected, others crowded into sheds and rummaged through the garbage, several — and the percentage had gone up — committed suicide, and Thérèse foresaw a wave of suicides in the years to come. What was there to do besides open shelters, fill the spaces with millions of beds, put up the homeless in government buildings if necessary , and here a newly reconstructed shelter was opening for Polydor, Abeille — there were already pots of paint, brushes, an easel in the studio and that drawing table, that perfectly mobile table that had been Thérèse's first purchase — Gérard, Doudouline, though it was still missing a staircase, a main entry, that Thérèse (but what naïveté, they were sure to make fun of their abode) would offer to all of them, but with no alcohol or smoking, no, they would never come, despite their financial difficulties, they would reject that life of balance and health, the moment would come that they would regret it. And there was always that satirical pamphlet that the computer faithfully displayed in which Thérèse accused the State, that unabashed .0114352 percent of the budget, and it was at that moment that the leaning roof returned to haunt her spirit obsessively. As for the gutter-pipe and the violent summer rains to come, this was a problem that she didn't know how to resolve, she thought as she drummed on the keyboard of her computer. Later she would arrange her files to avoid thinking about the things that demanded all her attention: the leaning of the roof, the gutter-pipe if it rained. But Thérèse had compiled so many diverse documents — delinquency, homelessness, adolescent suicide — that she no longer knew how to arrange them, her Master's thesis was lying on her desk too, in an office that was still unfinished, the beams waiting in the hallway. And suddenly, the sexism of that expression used for the homeless shelters irritated her, men were opening what they called "Father's Houses." There it was, thought Thérèse, a sovereign disdain for the homeless themselves who were already rejected by the society into which they had been born. By what clerical authority did this father suddenly appear, with his oppressive protection, his suspicious paternity? If they had said "Mother's Houses" it would have been a joke, a woman counted so little when she defended those worse off than herself. And then the computer, instrument of precision, thought Thérèse, hadn't it been invented by men and only for men, their business communications and transactions? Could anyone have imagined that the situation would become such a serious, urgent problem, the situation, unique for Thérèse, of the homeless aged fifteen to eighteen, that a woman, like a man, would have in her car, for the new era of human communication, a network system for emergency assistance calls, cellular messages hooked up to the computer that allowed lives to be saved? And those wood chips on the floor, wouldn't they have to be swept up, put to the side, they would provide fuel for the kitchen stove in the fall? What was Abeille doing with Paula anyway, a woman thirty years older than she was who smoked, drank too much, polluted the atmosphere with her cigarettes, coughed in the morning as she went to work, her briefcase under her arm? That would come to a bad end, she didn't know the statistics on cancer, and that desperate carnal quest of Paula's, whether the women were from her side of the tracks or not, she rushed in, was also a threat to mental and physical health, and Thérèse had blushed, though there was no one around to see her, she still blushed at the memory of Paula's hand on her fleshy thigh, after she had come back from jogging on the mountain, Paula's long fingers wandering underneath her blue striped shorts. How that expert caress had troubled her, unnerved her, once, when she was preparing to rejoin Abeille who was waiting for her at the bottom of the hill standing next to her bicycle. "Ah! Abeille's good times," and Paula had laughed as she said, "But that doesn't mean anything, what are you so frightened of?" Paula's astounding sexuality seemed to fill the air along with the smoke from her cigarettes, the digestion of her copious meals — so lacking in vitamins, thought Thérèse. Some part of Thérèse had been violated by Paula, she thought, even if Paula was a symbol for all of them of the struggle for the liberation of women during an obscure period of their history. It was Paula too who had one day invited Johnie, then Gérard, Doudouline to cross the lake at Sophie's in her canoe, Paula and her more or less consentual rapes, Thérèse thought, her laughter in the summer air, or her controlled sobs, but who didn't want a ride in the canoe with Paula? Paula the great liberator of the neighborhood! It was when they were coming back, the oars rippling the water, the appearance of a crimson face, a quickly repressed smile as they walked towards the bank that betrayed for one after the other their complicity in this loss of innocence with Paula. As for Paula, she docked her canoe and waited for the sunset, standing on her long legs insolently, thought Thérèse, and continuing to pollute the atmosphere with her cigarettes, yes, that caress had been excruciating, like an insult to Thérèse's modesty. Good, she ought to remember that, too, and write about it: A hotel room cost almost a hundred dollars a night in the States, a bed in a hostel barely twenty. They arrived from everywhere, from the north, our Ethiopians. For them, no employment, no stability except for the street. Yes, but the way the girls lived, never looking for work, Gérard sometimes stealing a steak from the supermarket, Polydor working in the bookstore only on Saturdays, they could easily find themselves in one of those shelters for the homeless, thought Thérèse, the Father's Houses, the Father's Hostels, lying against the very breast of their charitable enemies, metamorphosed into debonair therapists, understanding priests.

Sophie looked at her watch, it would soon be time to go back — and it displeased her to leave this way, towards the furnace of the streets on Sunday night in summer, and to soon be overheating in the stifling wings of the theater where she would be crushed by everyone — the girls would certainly forget to water the plants, they would scratch her crystal glasses with their pointy fingernails, because they always drank a bit too much in the evenings, break her porcelain, what did they do all day in the country besides expose themselves to the sun almost naked on the terrace or read in the shade of the birch and cedar trees? Sophie was appalled by those bikinis that concealed nothing, not even that patch of Doudouline's rosy flesh that she would have preferred not to see, and Polydor who was reading Saint John of the Cross in her indecent panties, her genitals open to the air, she was so relaxed, and Sophie had been stunned as if she had been struck with nausea, as Doudouline was singing, humming a melody that seemed inappropriate in light of Baby Doc's beaches. This nausea tormented Sophie so powerfully that she told Doudouline to be quiet, but Doudouline answered that she needed her mother's piano to write her music. "My piano again? Yesterday my car, when are you going to stop begging, all of you, children?" And even as she was grumbling, Sophie felt a vague sense of guilt at having sent Doudouline on vacation — even if it was to care for her bronchitis — to an island where a terrorist regime was in power, it was because of the reduced prices, of course, the mild tropical climate, the beaches, but most mothers would not have sent their daughters to one of the most famine-stricken countries of Latin America, she thought, and now Doudouline, with her grating melody marked with the bitterness of the first shock that life gives you, Doudouline remembered, didn't she, with her angelic voice that was tormenting the air, how we were vulnerable despite ourselves to dictators that made all the world uninhabitable? If Doudouline hadn't seen the massacres of the *tontons macoutes*, they had pervaded the air she breathed, stretched out on the sand between the Atlantic and the Caribbean, as she let herself be anesthetized by the white light of crime in which she floated under the layer of suntan lotion that covered her skin, there she was, among others, on an island where torture was currently being practiced and she knew that at that time a dictator called the Baby had taken refuge on the Côte d'Azur where he bemoaned his exile in his city of millionaires. Everywhere he went, from the Côte d'Azur to the Maritime Alps, his crimes followed him, this didn't stop him from circulating. A trail of blood ran between the Atlantic and the Caribbean where Doudouline had gone to cure her bronchitis, the blood ran in the trees too, in the field where the rice, the tobacco, the corn grew, whether Sophie consented to it or not, Doudouline had witnessed all of these horrors right next to her at the time of her bronchitis. Then Sophie had put on her city clothes to go, and at the moment she was looking for her car keys in her purse she had glimpsed her reflection in the rearview mirror and seen that wrinkle at her mouth that was often the sign of her irritation. And far off, behind the glow of her red hair, she had seen Doudouline and Polydor reading under the trees, her birches, her cedars as Doudouline's annoying song drifted up, and she had thought with a mixture of maternal pride and fear: Yes, but there is always the future to fix everything.

Part 2

The Threshold of Pain

Johnie, Polydor, Doudouline were together again in Abeille's living room. Shouldn't they call the police? Johnie was asking. Where was Gérard? No one had seen her for several months. "Most likely at a gay bar in Provincetown where she's been spending her nights dancing," answered Abeille acidly, for what could be more unjust than that concern they all felt about Gérard, who had left while she, Abeille, who had come back, they barely noticed, was standing up in her blue painter's smock near her easel on which she had yet to put a canvas as she was vacillating between several projects: Hadn't the time come to express her most violent sentiments, her exclusion from this planet, for even if you could still see the stars moving in the night sky, the dawn of Abeille's generation was not visible, she thought, it was a generation that was cast to the side under the feet of the avid, hysterical competition of the businessmen who directed the world. If there was no room in the world for Abeille, there was no room for the fish and birds that were killed by acid rains, or perhaps she would draw like Paula, with no colors, using blacks and dark browns or perhaps .... It wasn't worth getting so worked up, losing sleep and appetite, not even opening a notebook as Johnie was doing, always at the window, her long back hunched in a sadness she did not explain to the others — yes, but in that black rests all the blackness of Paula's soul, thought Abeille, and we live surrounded by living, colorful planets, the planets twinkle and we burn out, thought Abeille, the trees, the leaves were seared with those autumn colors that announced the winter in the streets, and so it was that nothing ever changed, under the cracks in the ceiling, under the burden of the grooves, in that living room where the girls continued to stagnate, thought Abeille, with their beers and the smoke from their cigarettes, especially Johnie who was corrupting the air in the room with her brown cigarettes that burned themselves out in her yellowed fingertips. An inevitable period of time had to pass here. Gérard, Gérard, wasn't she free, as she had always been? Why all this sudden anxiety, she would come back when she was hungry, she hadn't yet been stabbed in a dark alley even when she was coming home at five in the morning. Her agile silhouette was well known in the neigh boring bars, however, but why not run away, why linger in a country, a city, where the poets, the writers, were dying, where the painters were despairing? Here, with all these cracks in the ceiling, these girls in the smoke, eternity hovered like low thunder, nothing but the plan to wait in boredom, for there could be no more illusions after that hallucination of colors in the trees and the sky, the night, the cold whose color could not be painted on a canvas, it was too opaque, too frozen, a substance so vile it caused the heart and circulation to stop, and Doudouline was scraping at her guitar as Polydor caressed her cheek with her kisses. Two, they were always two, while Abeille had failed so many times to be two and never was — couldn't Thérèse name almost two hundred encounters, including the men? — even when they saw each other every day, they still wrote poems to each other, songs they slipped under the pillow at night: My darling Doudouline, my dear love Polydor, my little Saint John of the Cross, could you bring me my breakfast in bed, go by the cleaners tomorrow for your Doudouline, and while these desperate babblings were going on Abeille was still hanging around Paula like the pyramids at Chichen Itza — and Paula slowly climbed them to the top — and when Thérèse had led her to the jars of gouache on the drawing table in a house, a studio that had been renovated for her, Thérèse's majestic arms hanging around her neck in that demand, "So now, do you want to live with me?" Abeille had understood that the joyful fate of a couple was already not for her, as Thérèse who had been an idealist and was not anymore, didn't smoke anymore, didn't drink anymore, would vacuum just when Abeille was busy painting or reflecting on something, wrote in the sea of files she had on her desk on the freaks, the drug addicts, the homeless, and was starting a dissertation in gerontology. She was a woman of the twenty-first century, thought Abeille, her planet was no longer appealing. Living with Thérèse, being two, would have been that, sharing her smiling, though objective or neutral (as everyone goes through it) humanitarianism for all unfortunates except for her, Abeille, living with the pre-occupations an d the grumblings of old age — Thérèse would have said "the psychological difficulties of the golden years" — and before those jars of gouache, the exquisite drawing table that docilely followed the movements of the painter's hand, Abeille had detested the art of painting that belonged only to Paula, her furious instruction, her rages or the bites her jealous suspicion drove her to when they made love. The couple was dead, defunct, and Johnie was saying that they ought to call Thérèse, as if this were one of Gérard's first flights — the police, no, said Polydor, this is our business, not theirs, they are present in our lives enough as it is. Thérèse was a reasonable woman, Johnie was saying, perhaps the only one among the girls in the group. Johnie turned her back on Abeille who was still standing next to her empty easel, the round, sensual planets would be red, black, hot blue, seen alone, silent in space, and the one surviving bird would be alone too on a branch at the side. Yes, but the problem with Gérard, thought Abeille, was that she had been spoiled by chivalric parents who had adopted her at an advanced age, by women who had ceaselessly paid homage to her, Gérard so seductive and loose, it was believed, carefree, with her impenetrable boyish allure beneath the black curls of her hair, dressed in her riding vests that her mother sewed for her, her superb costumes that were tailor-made, Gérard who would be haunting the Club in her dinner jacket with the red silk lining. She would have to come back, she'd never leave for so long without telling the girls, how selfish! And Thérèse's arms were again surrounding Abeille's shoulders with their tenderness, sitting straight up at the drawing table where the jars of gouache sparkled, how had such a charming twosome been broken up? Was it that new technical volubility of Thérèse's that had so hurt Abeille? And the twenty-first century with no fairy? Didn't Thérèse belong more to what she called "collectives" — reflections on ethics, reflections on the flagrant discrimination against the visible minorities, the minority she didn't seem to realize she was part of — more than to Abeille to whom she had just offered herself with the majesty of her heavy arms around her neck? Polydor was enough, wanting to reform the social order, reforming it already with her lectures at the university, among her dusty theologians who had never realized that women could think and be, much less Polydor, whose sex was undefined for her own good, or undefinable for the good of all, Polydor who was going to be a gay priest and a woman on top of that, how unfortunate, had already experienced her agony before the drawing table, the jars of gouache, and that oppressive memory of Paula painting in the depths of her basement below the light bulb that illuminated her large, creative hands, stained with the ink and paint that often appeared at night in Abeille's dreams, the alluring ghost of Paula repeating "Art is finished, there will be no more, think about something else." Abeille, yes, it must have been then that the thought of becoming two with a Thérèse who had metamorphosed into a computer, reserving for Abeille all the treasures of her goodness and the marvels of modern technology, whether she was speaking or writing, that the marriage with the dreamed-of soul had disappeared. And Gérard went out a lot when she was still with us, in her tight pants, her elegant Saturday night sweaters, or the sloppiness of her Mickey Mouse T-shirt under her dinner jacket, she went out a lot, and there, too, dancing with one partner and then another in the moonlight, the good life, thought Abeille, near the sea, Gérard's fleeting moments of joy, far away, the nights she didn't sleep, yes, but she never drank alcohol, and what other things did she do to make up for it? And Abeille felt those sensations of envious revulsion that she did not like to observe in herself: It was so ugly to leave in a car with another group, Americans, to do this to us like that, without saying anything, for an unknown destination. And Polydor had filled her cupboard with canned food, fed the cat, brought Doudouline's gold-spangled dress for her concert — gold everywhere, said Doudouline, even in my hair — back from the cleaners, and Johnie was offended that they had already forgotten Gérard to talk about the dress that Doudouline was going to wear, but so it was that nothing ever changed, not for better or for worse, thought Abeille — ennui pressed itself into you — and again she envied Gérard who hadn't invited her to take part in her pleasures there, all those opportunities at every door, bars that stayed open all night, swimming in the green water when it was warm in summer, and those women all around, come from everywhere, but there was one that week at the Club, the medical student, a brain, it seemed, already in research and giving lectures, but when would she see her again? The cracks in the ceiling only got wider and time stood still with those images: Paula painfully descending the steps of the El Castillo pyramid or drinking her tequila under the burning sun a few hours before throwing herself into the waves and a man stretching out his hand to her above the storm and shouting "Ich komme, ich komme," it was a picture of demonic strength imprinted on Abeille's flesh like one of Michelangelo's pictures below the vaults of the Sistine Chapel, but the hand of God was as capable of destroying as of creating, and even if Paula had not perished at that instant, wouldn't something else, in herself, have destroyed her, the audacity of her confidence, her headstrong will?

It is impossible to heal flesh that has been wounded, no one can be consoled for the absence of the dead, thought Johnie, standing at the window, in the blaze of

autumn reflected in the window behind the curtains —
that sentence she had written in her essay that morning
evoked the mournful eyes of Radclyffe Hall who had
crossed through the shadows, the eyes of the writer that
had been so vulnerable to the light during the great sufferings that preceded her death — those shadows, our prejudices, our childish fears, or that era of persecution
Radclyffe Hall had foreseen that we were living in, and all
these thoughts of Johnie's were lost, latent, among her
nightmares, the image of Gérard struggling to swim in the
black waters of a stagnant pond teeming with carp or
those monstrosities that we only see in our dreams,
swarming around us in the greenish hunger of crocodiles
and fins; Johnie's own hunger striding up a series of rectangular staircases that glowed pearly white, the steps
vibrating under Johnie's feet as she called "Gérard,
Gérard," with no one to hear her. That vision seemed more
frightening than the other, with the shaky steps of the
staircase, the rectangular forms she could not avoid, and it
was in that dream that Johnie had gathered white roses
and dead roses. She could still feel the velvety touch of
those roses that were not alive, white everywhere, which
in dreams, when they were artificial, symbolized the
detachment, the abandonment of life. But how could she
console herself for the absence of the living also, for perhaps Gérard had simply left, as she often did in the summer, ran off in her red plastic shoes seeking the novelty of
her games with the girls who had come from the other
side of the frontier. For some time, she hadn't been coming
back to Johnie's place at daybreak except to tumble into
her bed fully dressed, and for Johnie, Gérard's brief periods of sleep, composed of something other than sleep, like
the fake roses, roses that didn't breathe, didn't live, looked

like a coma, Gérard's irregular breathing had terrified her so many times that she had called a doctor. Then suddenly, when she was about to be cured, Gérard wasn't there any more, there was no trace of her in Johnie's apartment. And Johnie had read those letters from Lynda in which "the wind was blowing in the Sahara," far away, and here, between the four walls where Johnie lived when she was alone, the wind was blowing in the Sahara, it continued to blow as she watched the purple autumn leaves falling the length of the window in Abeille's living room. Lynda had traveled the Mediterranean coast with her prince, an engineer or gas dealer, thought Johnie, she had seen immense beaches of fine sand, visited the holy cities of Montay, Idriss, Meknes and Volubilis with him, she had seen eucalyptus too, oleander that turned toward the sea, she had done archery, horseback riding, seen the Valley of the Casbahs, and suddenly there was nothing but Lynda separated from all these fabulous sites, Lynda listening to the wind blow in the desert, writing to Johnie that it was cold at night alone there, with the sounds of Moslem prayers, all those men prostrated before Allah in the city as well as the country, it was cold at night with the wind blowing in the desert, and did Johnie know that there had once been a mosque here with domes supported by twenty thousand columns and eighty bronze doors and millions of lamps that burned all night long. Here, there would be the most marvelous mosque in all the world, and had Johnie finished her novel, started her essay, was she still going out at night with her brother Gérard who was a woman? And the wind was blowing in the desert, thought Johnie, and there would be bronze doors, marble columns, and each person would have to pay for it in blood, and like that hidden angel that had ordered the mother of Mohammed to carry her son around the world, an invisible angel would one day guide Lynda back home where she would be with Johnie again, Lynda promised, "I'll come back soon, Johnie. I'll come back soon, this man, if you only knew, nothing but men everywhere and all I have is you, Johnie" — and Johnie's heart beat so hard she thought it would burst — she was going to come back, she said, that man had deceived her, but after that there would be another one, and then another one, Lynda had never lived without them, and far away Lynda's eyes swept from the bronze doors of the mosque to the skyscraper erected on rotten foundations among the mangy dogs and children next to the mosques that sounded their last trumpets in the evening air. And suddenly Johnie felt as if she were with Lynda like before, as she was seeing reality through her eyes, though everything Lynda wrote hurt her, from the exhausted donkeys dying in agony at the side of the high-way to the dozens of stuffed birds in a cage at the market — a European woman had looked at the cage and said "the poor dears" — or children that sold their mothers in the streets, the cruelty inflicted on the lambs, the horses during a slaughter. Sorrow ran in the clumsy pages in which Lynda spoke so little of herself, her grief, her betrayal, but they were so close, thought Johnie, that Lynda was beginning to see others as Johnie saw them. But when she wrote "The sun is out ... it's three in the afternoon ... it's not raining anymore and I hear the knife-sharpener going by," it was like the words of the European woman, punctuated with a tone of powerless pity — "the poor dears" — uttered before the birds and their songs that would be slaughtered for the evening feast, and who was this banquet for, Lynda had asked as the birds screamed themselves hoarse, crowded against each other.

And a veil of pardon that came not from Allah but from the rain in the sky ought to stretch itself over the earth, over all those sacrifices to cynical and vengeful divinities, thought Johnie, yes, that had to be the sign, with Lynda's meditation in the sun at three o'clock, that a celestial rain would come to purify, with the knife-sharpener, all that blood that would soon be spilled on the plains, in the fields, in the cities, and in the desert where the wind blew.

Then Abeille had put a canvas on her easel, spreading her palette and brushes around her on the table — Paula in her choirboy blouse that barely covered her naked buttocks would show her the etching of the black burned tree, Paula getting ready to go out, in her somber detective's trench coat, with her briefcase stuffed with drawings under her arm, violently snatching away the walkman, Abeille's sacred walkman, Madonna, Tina Turner, yes, for Paula the world was collapsing by the hour, and Abeille's hand trembled as it came into contact with the brushes, but she saw the alignment of the planets the way she intended to paint it, with black space all around, and when she was about to draw the bird that had survived the nuclear holocaust on its branch — this was why, she thought, she always put all the planets to the side as if they were drifting alone out towards infinity — she said to herself that, like the bird, she ought to hang onto her branch, what she still had before the event of the nuclear holocaust, before the earth exploded and went drifting around. She could love, sing like Doudouline, paint or express herself with colors, the colors of radioactive fallout on the earth, her isolation in paradise, though it was a paradise shot through with morbid omens, and since Thérèse had opened her house to everyone, you could hear her everywhere singing the praises of her vegetarian dishes. Abeille's body was obstructed with toxins, lucerne and dandelion, a mild purifier, would save her. Incredible, after all the drinking she had done, that she didn't have cirrhosis already, crammed with cholesterol at Paula's table, she needed Thérèse, her advice, her ascetic principles, in order to reconstitute herself normally. Sooner or later Abeille would have stomach ulcers, she should eat lucerne, and if she was so dependent on sex to function (it was bad for the health, and Abeille already had circles under her eyes), it was really indispensable to her, but she would live longer if she made love less, contrary to popular belief, she should munch on celery sticks throughout the day, celery was a known aphrodisiac and also helped to eliminate toxins, of which Abeille had many, said Thérèse, who ran her three kilometers every morning, her forehead high under the elastic band that held her hair back, she ran without a walkman, thought Abeille, this in itself was a generation gap, without keeping Michael Jackson's shrill music in her ears, and that daily run on the banks of a river covered with filth seemed like a futile gesture to Abeille, lacking in imagination like those meals that Thérèse perfected for her homeless people. Then Abeille had seen that golden light undulating on the canvas, in the white square where the canvas was still intact, the light of autumn that came from the window where Johnie was standing in silence, and she said to herself that she suddenly felt the absence of Gérard, it was there in her soul, in her heart like a hole in the core of her being, suddenly: Where was Gérard? Where was Gérard? It came to her with the light that undulated on the canvas, that question that had no answer, for Abeille had just sensed it, Gérard would never come back.

And Johnie again saw Marianne typing a letter under her wide-brimmed hat on that beach, under the sky ploughed with warplanes next to the Pacific where they had gone swimming, gone to sleep, wiped out by the heat, lying next to each other, and it suddenly seemed inconceivable to her that Marianne was in Jerusalem opening a museum, gathering together artists from all countries, talking about Chagall in her letters, at a time when Johnie had seen that morning as she walked to Abeille's house, on the walls in the slums of the city, those words written in big black letters: "Israel, assassin." Yes, unbeknownst to us was unfolding — and this was inconceivable for the innocents of the earth — a torrent of atrocious events, an onslaught of fire and blood that our eyes lacked the courage to see, for while Marianne contemplated works of art, hung them on immaculate walls, became attached to an artist's vision in which the purified life of his or her tragedies looked like a golden spoon, lions and lambs that fought no more in the peace of the stained glass windows, the silence of the cathedrals, the museums, all the while stone-throwers were dying every day, come from refugee camps to the beaches of the Middle East where massacres were to follow, bloody atonements of little concern to the generals and sons of generals who had provoked them, they came without weapons, supplied with rocks, bandages over their eyes like a cloud of blind doves and they wouldn't be going back to their mothers in the evening as an army patrol had shot them all down and they were bleeding, they were bleeding, though their mothers, their sisters had long ago ceased to cry for them, they were still bleeding among the stones they had thrown on the sand of the beaches, in the barbed wire that their clothing, already in shreds, was attached to, bits of it embedded in their flesh, they were bleeding black blood in those letters that had been written during the night on the walls in the slums, right near Abeille's house, but for Marianne who had written to Johnie, there were no murdered stone-throwers, only Jerusalem, the happy Jerusalem that she'd long held in her heart, and that thought terrified Johnie, both for Marianne and herself, for it suddenly seemed to her that history had always been "decided" by men, founded on an ideal of armed revenge that belonged only to them, women, even when they were losing husbands and children, acted as if history hadn't been their concern and contributed to a passivity responsible for their own agony, as Marianne was doing: Her actions suddenly seemed condemnable. As the lion and the lamb nestled together below the same rays of divine fire in Chagall's stained glass windows, Marianne took over Chagall the way she had taken over an island in the Pacific, with her gardener, her masseur and the black chauffeur she gave orders to in the morning to wash his car for her parties in the evening. Like a baron or prince she ruled over her collections of paintings, galleries, wasn't it possible to buy everything, thought Johnie, from the tears of Van Gogh as he ran crazy though the streets of Arles or painted among the shepherds in the fields, on the edge of insanity, to that cut-off ear that had left its scarlet stain on a painting? The woman who had written to Johnie from a city whose name in Hebrew was "Peace will come" didn't hear the groanings of war below the chants from the mosque, though she was a woman endowed with great sensitivity, meditating in a graveyard at the tombstones of those she had lost, respectfully saluting the rabbi in her prayers. It seemed to her moreover that victory and justice could only come from those young men wandering in the street in their military uniforms or standing vigil, one hand already resting on their bayonets under the vault of the olive trees. Johnie, in her youth, Marianne wrote to her, could understand nothing of these people who possessed the truth, a piece of divine revelation on the earth which had to be defended at any price, and the soldiers were advancing with their tanks under the cypresses, they were advancing with their troops and jeeps on the fine sand towards those stone-throwers come from their refugee camps in their vermin-infested clothes, and how sad it would be if they didn't go back to their mothers in the evening, how sad it would be if they were killed in the morning. Marianne, a good, charitable woman, cried for her own dead, for there was a price to pay for liberty, an unspeakable price when paradise was stolen in hell. And Johnie remembered her walks with Marianne along those paths of white pebbles near the sea when a kitten lurking in the bushes had attacked a seagull with one bite, she saw the feet still pointing toward the sky below the bloodstained feathers as Marianne said to her in a calm voice, "Don't be so upset, it's just a life coming to an end." Johnie heard that same voice, implacably serene or calm in the face of death, as between the lines she read: "One stone-thrower a day dies here, shot down by our guards, but there's nothing I can do, nothing I can do, ah! if only you were next to me ...." But Johnie thought that she would never again be next to Marianne, on her island or in any other place, if this drama of invisible blood that was expanding every day, from one wall to the other in the Holy City where peace was *not* coming, was already separating them. There was a secret war between Marianne and Johnie that Marianne seemed not to be conscious of, thought Johnie. Marianne, despite a physical attraction to Johnie that she did not deny, for it did her honor, didn't it, and hadn't she paid the price, inviting Johnie into her world of luxury, Marianne unconsciously treated Johnie the way she had treated the black "boy" she whistled to to bring her a screwdriver on a platter, what's more, thought Johnie, she was Marianne's Arabian servant leaning towards the sun, for at the bottom of her soul, though she was attracted to her, sometimes going so far as to admire Johnie because she was learning Greek to read Sappho in the original, Marianne looked down on Johnie and her difference that *must not* be seen. Perhaps Johnie's discomfort had begun when Marianne had said "vous" when speaking to her. More than a sign of respect, oddly, Johnie had sensed in that a certain condescension that had displeased her, that "vous" not only cut her off from the society Marianne belonged to, but that "vous" among caresses and games of the flesh also masked a truth — or a reality — that Marianne refused to see in herself. Later, when she was back from New York, hadn't Marianne written to Johnie that she was going to send all her letters back, because, she said, "My husband must know nothing about all this, I've already told you, I love my husband, and my son, who's actually studying in England, must know nothing about it either." It was then that Johnie had felt the whip of hardship that turned her towards the sun, although that lash, administered with a distracted hand by Marianne, who was thinking foremost about her own business, who was not a sentimental woman (didn't what she shared with her husband take precedence over all her own pleasures?), had given her a much-needed jolt, she had rediscovered, with Marianne's rejection, her Angel of Solitude that had always been waiting for her in the shadows, as if to say to her, "So when are you going to defend your rights? You,

an unarmed soldier, when are you going to stop camou-
flaging yourself in the foliage that shelters you among the
girls of the group, when are you going to be yourself in
the eyes of the world, in resplendent clarity?" That letter
from Marianne ended with words Johnie had already
heard: "You are a lesbian and, despite my attachment to
you, I am not. We'd be best off forgetting this episode."
The war, then, was frank and open, thought Johnie, you
could have counted the casualties, heard the tolling bell
that forever separated them, Marianne and Johnie, Johnie
and Marianne who never should have met, never should
have kissed, never should have loved each other, with the
sword of the Angel of Solitude between their bodies that
embraced but never merged. And at that moment, Johnie
began to think how much that word "lesbian" was the
bearer of defamatory libel in the eyes of others, that
despite the most important revolution of her era, it held
the same insulting connotations, shameful scorn as it had
at the time of Radclyffe Hall. This was why, finding no
other words, they had become, rather than sad in their
burden and rejection, gay creatures, freeing themselves
from a language that the presence of racism and sexism
had long ago exhausted and damaged. All of this Johnie
would write later in her essay, she thought, although the
thought of the Gay Era, after its few bursts of liberation
that were quickly censured by religions as well as by
governments, suddenly seemed to open up to her, and
whether they admitted it or not, the Church, like the State,
or the Churches and the States, could not but rejoice, for
finally such punishments, punishments they'd dreamed of
for centuries, were returning a bit of order to all this chaos,
sex was death, sex was castigation — during the era of the
Pink Triangle, the Triangle of calamity that had sent

millions of men into crematoriums, into the prisons of Siberia — at the moment that Johnie was going to write her essay they were being beaten in Siberia at dawn, an unforeseeable revolver shot to the neck, thus avoiding, for humane reasons, they said, the anguish of the death penalty. The Pink Triangle was no longer pinned on outside but inside, in the flow of infected blood through the veins, blood composed of HIV, sweat, tears, sperm, the new victim of the Pink Triangle withered away and died in this blood, altered by the presence of viruses, a gradual decline as stigmatizing as lightning disintegration. And the saunas and pools were emptying out, the hospitals, the houses, the streets, the schools, those branded with the Pink Triangle were being erased, dying, chased out of the places they lived, the houses of their happiness where their lovers, children, or mothers waited to be tagged also, inside, crucified wordlessly, or in other cases, those marked with the Pink Triangle were isolated from others, an emaciated little black girl in her pink tutu, playing with a ball in her plastic bubble, exiled from the hospitals, prisoners of the dying, those who were still alive; Johnie's dignity lay in enduring the eternity of the Pink Triangle on her body that had not yet been named, though it had been said that she was lesbian or gay, her dignity lay in knowing that she did not yet have a name that was distinguished or distinguishable, but stranded among her contemporaries that bore the Pink Triangle, her conquest of liberation in life, like her fragile conquest of life itself, had never been so threatened.

§

And Polydor had cleaned Gérard's room, opened the blinds that had been closed for so long, remade the bed with a firm hand, no wrinkles in the bedspread she pulled over the flannel sheets, the squishy pillows Gérard liked in the winter — though she had a habit of throwing her pillows against the wall when her pills didn't help her to sleep in the morning, or when she had nightmares wide awake like that too realistic, powerful hallucination in which she saw herself fluttering from wall to wall, perched like a bat or a spider in a splintered, worm-eaten window from which she could see the destruction that was the world, nothing left but a few people wandering around in their fur coats under collapsing porticoes among the smoking wreckage. But she was sure of it, the world had been destroyed, Gérard's bed was floating alone in a bright stream of light as Polydor swept away the acrid dust that covered the furniture with her rag, respectfully uncovering the space Gérard had inhabited during the night that she would return to soon, today, perhaps tomorrow, because one of her hairs was still stuck like a black silk thread in her brush and in the photos from her childhood she had glued to her wall she was still smiling, revealing the whiteness of her protruding teeth, holding up a rabbit or another animal her parents had just given her. Here she was on a boat on her father's lap, or here on horseback in a riding habit, again with him, was this the same Gérard, sitting high up in the air, who now spent her nights in the bars? thought Polydor. God is waiting for you in the Anglican Church, her professor had said to her, and Polydor had thought, there are other theologies, Islam, Judaism, why limit yourself to the most ignorant, intolerant church, where Saint Thomas Aquinas followed you into your bedroom, where a phallic league decided whether or not we should have children after they had deflowered us, and that papal gynecological lamp that thrust its way into our uterine canals, if Doudouline could only question herself, but no, her music, Gounod and her rock opera, she undulated beneath her nightgown at night, round, hot, voluptuous, a Renoir, my Doudouline, and Gérard was still smiling her bucktoothed smile in her childhood photos, the black silk of her hair clung to the brush on the chest near the bed, Gérard would be back any second now, thought Polydor. And if God was waiting for Polydor in the Anglican Church, why wasn't he giving her a sign? What would become of all those students who were rushing for their diplomas, what would they be after they had their degrees in theology, waiters in restaurants or unemployed, biting their nails in front of the television? God's positions were all occupied by God himself, those decrepit old professors waiting for their retirement, immersed in their studies of religion, pontificating in praise of man, for no one spoke of woman because of her vices as well as her virtues. There was no place among them for Polydor, who knew that God would never give her a sign, for Polydor had never tolerated the idea of God, the God of erudite old age that held every position in the university, numbing the discordant spirit of the young, any more than she tolerated man and the unpleasantness of his theology and philosophy. She was floating alone then, from the warm arms of Doudouline to the obscure night of Saint John of the Cross.

If she faithfully followed her professor's advice, a woman who, despite everything, had been ordained as a priest, an impressive feat in itself — "Read Saint John of the Cross, you'll see," she'd said, "God will give you a sign through this song of love," and ever since, Polydor had been waiting for that sign from God that always failed to appear, except that the photo of Gérard smiling her buck-toothed smile, with the rabbit she was holding lovingly close to her suddenly inflicted in Polydor a singular distrust of all those signs that came from heaven — if Polydor had luck on her side she too would be ordained one day, she could finally sow the seeds of rebellion among women and gay priests, for there were many of them, or else she would be made to keep quiet, she would receive a letter from her bishop begging her to do penance, wash and care for the sick and the old, and a stream of bright light fell onto Gérard's bed, even onto the fine silk of her hair in the brush, as if that were a sign from heaven she ought to be suspicious of, thought Polydor. And suddenly Polydor felt that everyone in that house demanded too much from her, the hungry cat that put its forefeet on the kitchen table and meowed shrilly, Abeille and her numerous emotional torments — now she was thinking about the medical student with the green eyes who'd been called a brain, when it would have been so much more simple to be faithful like most people — Johnie and her fits of writing, yes, but when she wasn't writing, her sanity paralyzed her for days, it was like a storm in the house, even the geranium going into tranquil hibernation in its pot was subject to the cigarette butts that Johnie feverishly crushed out in its leaves, in the soil that was too often dry. And now Doudouline was calling Polydor, in the middle of her voice exercises, the zipper on the back of her gold lamé dress had just jammed, she was going to be late for her afternoon rehearsal with her mother before the evening concert. Polydor, however, was well-acquainted with Sophie's startling unpredictability. Wasn't she known for her legendary discipline during rehearsals, what was Polydor doing in Gérard's room which was closed, and hadn't Abeille slept somewhere else again that night, hadn't she met yet another woman, a brain in science or in math? No, said Polydor, a doctor. For the moment, Abeille was here at her canvas painting, and Polydor thought as she zipped Doudouline up the back — Doudouline shivering with cold beneath the silky material — that even if she were not the mistress of God, as if Saint John of the Cross had been her lover at the time he was writing his enraptured hymns in prison, at least she was here, keeping her vigil, the woman who belonged to everyone, from the wailing cat — though it was ready to bite whenever anyone played with it — that she carried around her neck, to Doudouline, Abeille, Johnie, Gérard whom she had rocked against her heart each in turn. That had to be the most imperiously divine thing on the earth, making sure the refrigerator was stocked every day, soothing the morose and often hurtful moods of her neighbor, then Doudouline pouted disdainfully looking at her own reflection in the mirror in the living room: How, she thought, did this immense creature come out of my mother's delicately plump body, slender though petite, while I'm curvy though thin? Polydor, who was telling her how beautiful she was, was rebuffed with one dry word; soon, and this was already making her nervous and irritable like Sophie, Doudouline would be breathing the somber perfume of backstage in the theater, the air that had always belonged to her, the stuffy air of the theaters, the rehearsal rooms, it was there, perhaps, that her bond with Sophie became strongest, thought Doudouline, deciding that she had slimmed down sufficiently to be accepted in the world of show business, but that part of her had gone away like the coral reefs in the sea with this diet, perhaps her majesty had resided in the ampleness of her form, as Polydor repeated to her so often, but Sophie, her fragile Sophie, her love, hadn't she crushed Sophie when she was born, or taken away with her, in her queenly vigor, Sophie's lust for life, mother and daughter? But the voice, the authority, the melodious power of Doudouline's voice, where did that come from? Definitely from Sophie's voice, which could subjugate crowds, whether she was performing Strindberg or another playwright, and where were women in all this, they were deprived of emotion, why did Sophie only perform the works of men, often men who were in their graves, no less, and out of breath, Doudouline arrived backstage where her mother was waiting for her, except for Sophie, who was always so impetuous, you might have thought that nothing was going to happen here tonight on that stage, still dark, from which Sophie, in high heels and a suit (why was she suddenly like all the others, like a stranger Doudouline had met on the street), was talking to the lighting technicians, wasn't she the only one who understood the subtlety of the lights that would shine that night around the blond head that sparkled with gold, a bit punk but certainly *à la mode*, around Doudouline's angelic face, for only angels didn't need makeup on-stage, and when the rock orchestra, only the guitar, the bass and the drums — she was still opposed to the flute, it wasn't Christmas time — began to make themselves heard, Doudouline's voice would be admirably supported. Doudouline was the heart that beat in her chest, the blood that coursed through her veins, not all the time, but, yes, this would be the grand moment of their union, these nightclubs, people drooling over their beers at their tables. Was that reassuring for the singers, the musicians, the actors? If Doudouline would move a bit forward, she had a heavy look about her, her dress was hugging her hips a bit too tightly, if she would move a bit closer to the light, yes, that was good, the reddish light tinted with black, and Doudouline looked, deceived, at the dark room of the nightclub, the gray panels of its walls, those musicians adjusting their screeching instruments in their jeans with the holes at the knees on the stage where Sophie was sharply giving orders left and right, nothing, nothing good could happen tonight in such an unhealthy place, thought Doudouline, vaporizing her lungs with the chemical mist of her aspirator, since her throat was constricted the way it was before every concert, but it was there, lurking within her, her Voice, which would soon have the room vibrating with its timbre at once cacophonous and melodic. "Be expressive," Sophie was saying, "with your body as well as with your voice, keep trying," and Doudouline thought about her contracted lungs, looked at her mother with submissive fear, yes Mother, yes Mother, but what's going to happen tonight? And suddenly Doudouline saw herself sitting on her father's lap, this one a French father, they were eating raw carrots at the time, Sophie went to get the water from the well, the eggs from the hen house, those playwrights' and actors' children would never go to school like other children, they would learn to read from the dictionary, they would have foreign fathers with shrill French accents, a father who had come back from Paris with Sophie and Strindberg and Doudouline had learned to read on his lap. All of

119

Doudouline's fathers would come to the theater tonight, who knows, they had left their communes long ago, only in the city could a man think and act — what good was it to discuss Nietzsche and Rousseau in the country, with only the birds to listen to you? — and taken with sudden nostalgia for their territory, Doudouline's fathers had gathered in the cities, the universities. The men Doudouline had known smudged with dirt, among their naked children in the fields, had since been parading around in skimpy suits, cloistered among their books in houses of affluence, the eggs they were going to gather in the hen house in the morning, like the cock's crow at dawn, were no more than distant memories, Doudouline's fathers had left the farm, the carrots and cabbage they'd eaten raw, for the city where they elegantly concerned themselves with the lofty affairs of the mind, writers, art critics, editors of famous magazines, seen on the terraces of cafés in summer, at the tables of the best restaurants in winter, men of taste and of letters, would come crawling tonight with their notebooks to that dark, seedy room where Doudouline would offer them the warm modulations of her voice, all she possessed in the world, that voice, while they had words, the words she had learned on her father's lap, the words of the writer, the art critic, which could very well destroy her that night, as Doudouline's fathers held a pleasing but volatile power. She had her father's blue eyes, thought Sophie as she led Doudouline towards the stage, below the reddish light tinted with black, and Sophie's nails dug energetically into Doudouline's suddenly moist palm, but the voice flowed from her, Sophie, Doudouline's exceptional voice, from her alone, her flesh, her blood, actresses, singers, mother and daughter — as for her son, he was the invisible burden of fallen motherhood, a thorn in her side, when you thought about it, running away with his father's Hermès suitcases on the very day of the divorce — in that family, but why were the father's eyes there, searching Sophie's soul from the benevolent face of her daughter, what could they be still reproaching her for, her ferocious independence, perhaps? She wanted nothing to do with a man who wrote all day in his house. Sulky, skeptical, hardened, he smoked his pipe as he wrote, piling up manuscripts that would never be published, held discussions with the men of the commune as she changed the children's sheets, sewed curtains, insulated the windows and doors against the winter cold. Strindberg, Rousseau, why that trembling, fleeting glance from Doudouline, why her father's eyes below her childlike eyebrows, and Sophie told Doudouline that she was carrying herself poorly, a bit more spirit, you see, one doesn't sing with her eyes lowered, let's go, band, start up again, and Doudouline shuddered as she listened to her mother, the thought of those eyes fixed upon her, Doudouline's father's blue eyes, Sophie mused, it was a sensation of a contact that was too intimate, so intimate as to be displeasing, or perhaps because Sophie had carried Doudouline for too much time, the captivity had seemed long, but she had no right to think that, Doudouline had been an adorable baby, so quickly adored on television with her blond hair and rosy cheeks — "Buy Caress soap, for baby" — and the son had come so soon after, the rehearsal rooms in winter, and Doudouline who had been heavy, so heavy, when she was about to be born, mother and daughter too, one stocky silhouette walking in the snow. Claudel, Strindberg, with Doudouline kicking in her belly, they were not performed anymore today, Sophie was going to the East, drugs, prostitution, what an environment! These playwrights were too audacious, especially with language, which they abused. Forcing oneself to speak badly tortured the mouth, even if Sophie had never had speech lessons like Doudouline — and even violin lessons with a teacher who came to the commune, when Doudouline had barely begun to walk — she hadn't been to the Conservatory like so many others, the theater was a men's institution where women went unnoticed, no one listened to what they had to say. In every way, Strindberg, Ibsen, Claudel did it for them, dictated that they feel this or that. Watch out! Perhaps one day Sophie would write for herself, she had her experiences to back her up, Doudouline, her delinquent son, and soon menopause, Doudouline's father's blue eyes were looking at Sophie, and now a wintry cold was descending on the city, even if it *was* still autumn it would soon be snowing onto the red trees that were losing their leaves in the wind, and they were all together again in Abeille's living room, Thérèse had abandoned the homeless for the day, Doudouline after the triumphant evening of her concert, but it had already been a long time, you would have said, and in winter tears seized you by the throat, thought Doudouline. Abeille was there, rigid against the mauve bottom of her canvas, Johnie, turning her back to t he window, was asking what they would do with Gérard, where she would make love, but no one answered, not even Thérèse, who was sitting below the glorious frame of the picture Abeille had painted of her, smiling in her bathing suit on a summer day, *Thérèse* or *The Splendors of Summer*, said anything, her face half-hidden in her hands in a defeated attitude she was rarely seen in, for it was true, as the computer spelled out, the Third World, the slow destruction of Lebanon, and closer to home, the great mobilization of police, judges trying every day to retrieve children that were missing or murdered, modern-day effigies draped in plastic shrouds, plucked with gloves out of closets in buildings, dismembered, raped, tortured by their fathers, their brothers, sometimes a friend of the family, and to think that since she'd come back at the end of the summer, Gérard was hiding nearby, in that ghetto with those girls. They would need that abominable fire to understand, all the ghettos that burned down one after the other, in the winter, she was nearby, at our door, that mobilization of men, each more sinister than the last, psychiatrists, judges, police had only their instincts regarding the disappearance of diaphanous bodies that had been raped, strangled. In the east of France a peasant killed two boys with his scythe after raping them because they had crossed his field. The mountain, she would be alright on the mountain, her red plastic shoes, themselves foolish in the middle of winter, I should have predicted, imagined, the girl who ran her thirty meters in Seoul, what a painful effort her victory was, her face and muscles contracted. And Johnie was still asking what they would do with Gérard, and Thérèse thought of the Norwegian athlete who had broken her right foot during the race. The way Gérard slid her feet over the skating rink of the streets in their plastic shoes, her slender ankles blue with the cold was foolish, too. The problem, girls, said Thérèse in a tone that seemed senten-tious to Abeille, is that Gérard didn't eat enough, and you see what happens when you don't eat enough. And Abeille pointed out to Thérèse that she was drinking her third cup of coffee in an hour and had started smoking again, which was no longer among her habits, it wasn't worth it to preach to the others, and Abeille thought that she no longer loved Thérèse because she criticized her, and it would be liberating to love Thérèse no longer, like a weight on her chest being lifted, a stain on her heart that was diminishing, so that only her heart would remain to be assaulted no more. And Gérard took up too much space in the smoky living room, thought Abeille, the one they had barely seen move when she was there, Gérard was suddenly reduced to so little in an urn, a vase sitting on the table. Gérard was stretching out everywhere in her dinner jacket, they could hear her walking, laughing, yawning, the tiniest breath, at dawn when she went to join Johnie in bed, they heard her, and Abeille saw a woman come into the room, no one else saw her for it was her mother, her mother dressed in her light-colored clothes that she was wearing under a shawl. The last times at the hospital, her mother would humbly ask her to move her bed closer to the window, yes, just a bit closer, but no one saw that, not even Johnie who was so attentive to everything and heard all noises of the soul, only Abeille knew that the dead had as many rights as the living, that they could appear and then leave again with repentant discretion the way they had come, it was like the dream Abeille had had during the night, she couldn't push the bed to the window, there was a deluge of blood onto the sheets, onto her mother's legs, the blood her father was continuously washing away, he'd been caring for his sick wife for months, and now it was time for her morphine, but that blood, all that blood, Abeille never should have seen it, for it was gushing putrid from her uterus even though Abeille's father, with sublime patience, kept washing it away, it was nothing, but there were many who died from this affliction, there would be piercing screams, Abeille never should have seen or heard but gone back to her homework, practice her scales on the maternal piano, the piano that belonged to the piano teacher who was also a composer, but a composer whose music would never be heard, confined to a hospital with that furious sound of the poisoned blood in her ovaries, in her uterus, a sound that now droned in Abeille's ears every month, she had to distract herself from that, escape it, but Abeille had a duty to perpetuate her mother's uncompleted fate, take it up again — her mother who had become her daughter — her mother who had suffered the adversities of an epoch of black hostility against all artists (but we were still in that epoch) that needed Chopin incarnated in the body of a woman, her mother who had been bled to death — that was the word that kept coming back to Abeille's mind — by adversities and cancer, maternity, the burdens of mater-nity had bled her mother dry, and looking at the cold white light outdoors, she had closed her eyes to the world. There were at least four ovations, thought Doudouline, four times I reappeared on-stage, and they kept shouting bravo, Mother, I've got to wait for Mother who'll be here any minute, she'll get us out of this situation smoothly, tears flowed from Doudouline's blue eyes: What are we going to do with Gérard? What are we going to do with Gérard? It was a short ceremony, I wouldn't have imagined it so short, in a few days it will be her birthday, us, another us that is departing, we'll do what we usually do, we'll give her a party, the age of twenty ought to be celebrated, all the others were able to make it to the door, why not Gérard, oh God, why not Gérard, she never slept at night, why did she go to sleep that night? Mother will be here any minute now, don't be nervous, girls, Polydor, get us something to eat, even Doudouline's fathers had applauded with their flashy hands, those cautious and suspicious men that night had applauded and shouted bravo, and Doudouline had bowed on the stage holding her enormous bouquet of roses to her heart like a doll, and suddenly Gounod's divine melody that she heard in her dreams at night fell silent, kept silent, Gérard was there, in the middle of the room, but it was no longer like it had been before, the red shoes they'd seen flashing in the sun, the shoes of the latest punk fashion — like the gold chain around Gérard's neck, the chain that united Johnie and Gérard, though Johnie had never appreciated the cross that dangled from it — the red shoes and the gold chain were still intact but slightly charred, and Gérard was still standing, one finger on her pouty lips in front of the blinds that hadn't been opened for several months, the blinds that would always be closed from now on. "And get all this smoke away from me, open the window!" said Abeille, "I want to paint, the sky, the trees, the leaves, all that is left before winter comes." And Paula shoved Abeille against the wall of her moonlit basement as the etchings dried out on a corner of the table in the pallid light from the bulb that lit up the dark, disturbing contours, violently embracing Abeille, wasn't she trying to suffocate her? No, thought Abeille, she had been wrong to arouse her jealous fury, to provoke her, Paula had taught her etching, stimulated her, henceforth she would finish all her paintings, take up her drawing courses conscientiously this time, everything that happened in that house, that smoky living room over the past few hours was unreal, phantasmic, like trying to find your way in the fog. And Abeille leapt with rage when she heard Polydor ordering pizza and French fries on the phone in a dry voice; it seemed impossible to her that Doudouline could eat pizza with anchovies like she did every day, by what scandalous physical mechanism was she repeating those same actions today? But Polydor reminded all of them that they hadn't eaten since the day before, and the cat was meowing at the door. And Doudouline said "It's not my fault that I'm hungry, anyway." She had placed the box of Kleenex near her and was wiping her eyes at intervals. On Baby Doc's beaches she had tanned to the sounds of the machine guns, the rifles, on Baby Doc's beaches, yes, but that cello solo was not percussive enough, Mother's right, at every fifth you must pierce their souls, but you're just barely touching them, they're going to go home and forget the whole thing, the old dictator is still on the Côte d'Azur, suddenly there was a more insistent vibrato, and even Father came to kiss me and say, and he didn't have to say this, "I swear in all honesty, you astonish me, my girl, yes, there is an idea running through, a social idea with political implications, I never would have believed it of you, I still imagine you on my lap like when I was teaching you to read, what rhythm, my dear, what a voice, you had me shaking in my seat, your mother's telling me that you're writing a rock opera, bravo!" And never had Doudouline seen her mother so radiant, how sad for Gérard — she started to cry with jerky sobs again, her breasts heaving under her silk blouse, watched Polydor who was petting the cat in the kitchen — yes, it was so sad, Sophie, as she stood in the shadows in the back of the theater, had never glowed so, thought Doudouline, her eyes shining with pride as she watched her daughter swinging her hips on stage in her gold lamé dress, there, it's good, she seemed to be saying, though she was quite nervous and couldn't stop pacing around the room, it's art, serious work. She had swapped her grey suit and high heels from that afternoon for a more youthful outfit of denim, her elegance was versatile, refreshing, thought Doudouline, and at that moment came the powerful, long-awaited vibrato, and mother and daughter exchanged a look of the same unmistakable gratitude; how sad for Gérard, yes, but why was she hanging out with those girls from Provincetown, why was she hiding in the ghetto with their group, it was a true betrayal, and Thérèse, who was drinking her fourth cup of coffee below Abeille's luminous painting, seemed to have changed, aged imperceptibly, revealing a forehead that already testified to the burdens of intelligence, and said to Abeille severely, "I don't understand you, opening beers on a day like today, when we've just attended such a painful ceremony with Gérard's parents." And Abeille thought of the girl with the green eyes who had smiled at her at the Club, she too had intelligence, the medical student would come see her paintings that week, fortunately love could go away like a stain on her heart diminishing in intensity, an ache in the chest subsiding, all that smoke in her living room, the unpleasant smell of beer, winter was beginning its sacrifices with our Gérard, its slaughterhouse, its massacres, a portrait of Gérard in her dinner jacket, her red shoes, her curls blowing in the wind, yes, but as for the shoes, they had been charred in one night, as for Gérard, as for Gérard, they would leave the blinds closed or perhaps move in with Thérèse, this was not the time to think about her, the brain with the green eyes, not the time at all, I ought to be ashamed, and everything was ready for the big trip, really everything, their suitcases in the hall, complete with tags from the airline with their names on them, they were going to leave like they did every year for the merciful skies of Florida, they were going to leave, and that telephone ringing in the middle of the night, some of the tenants had been able to wake up and get out in time, others hadn't, not Gérard, she was too sluggish, our daughter, sluggish? The oxygen hadn't arrived on time, she couldn't have been sleeping, she had just come back, laughing and staggering, her landlady had told the reporters, these young people today live with no principles, laughing and staggering on the dilapidated stairs, taking refuge in unsanitary lodgings where they did drugs, injected themselves with needles, and there had to be orgies going on up there, she heard them whispering till dawn. And Gérard's parents, delicate creatures whose foreheads were now covered with a velvety white down, would never go to Florida again now, would no more cultivate their garden in the summertime, thought Thérèse, for they had been deprived of their reason to live, Gérard, that pile of ashes had been there on the horizon, below which the rabbit had been buried, and now Gérard, what day was it that Gérard had tried on her dinner jacket? Her fingers, Gérard's fingers stroking her mother's balding skull, fragile as the skull of a newborn, for Thérèse had held so many of those little old men in her arms, fragile underneath the sparse hair, as her mother hemmed the bottom of her pants, and the dinner jacket with the red silk lining had been reduced to ashes too, incinerated, and her parents had seemed lost as they followed the service, such a simple, sober ceremony, they too, however, had been burned, along with the dinner jacket with the red silk lining, and silently the black curls of Gérard's hair sank into the flames, leaving nothing but an odor of sulfur and putrefaction. That crown of dark hair that fanned out on the pillow where Johnie and Gérard rested their heads next to one another in one joyous diffusion. The suitcases were still waiting for them in the hall, but they knew that they would not be leaving that year, they would never again leave their house, their garden, there were too many ashes, too m any ashes all around. And Polydor saw all those dirty dishes that it was time to wash and as she plunged her hands into the soapy water she thought about that contemporary mystic who had said on television that "God is the other, the face of the other, God is no more than that." What were you supposed to do when the face of the other disappeared into the ashes? Where did you go to find God? And the face of God so loved for his grace and beauty vanished in the flames, and the fire, the cold, the snow trampled it mercilessly, the time of a blaze that had devastated everything, the sky had opened onto Gérard's suddenly absent face, God smiling above our miseries, before the fire and the arrival of the red firetruck, which bore the words "air supply," though air would never again enter Gérard's lungs, while the emergency lights flashed in the snow that was starting to fall in big wet flakes, the cold must have been what surprised Gérard, her feet bare in her plastic shoes, the walls had collapsed in the explosion, but it was such a muffled explosion that Gérard hadn't heard it, the cold was what surprised Gérard when she fell fully dressed onto her bed, the cold had suddenly imprisoned her, captured her alive. And on the street, the grocer's son jumped off his bike, climbed the stairs with the pizza and a case of beer under his arm and everyone went to sit down or eat, and what would Sophie say when she saw all this chaos, thought Doudouline as she licked her fingers, she'd probably say that Gérard had made a mistake in drinking six cognacs before going to bed that night, she was allergic to alcohol, had never drunk it before, it all started there, when you drank, you see, hadn't Doudouline noticed that her father was abusing alcohol, hadn't she noticed the night of the concert, how sad for Gérard, I'm so hungry, I can't hold back any longer, Sophie had seen things in the East of which Strindberg would not have approved, those boys, those girls who sold their bodies, and that wasn't all. Those girls could never leave her in peace, and now Gérard, no, it was too much, she'd been dreaming of a nice weekend in the country, and now Gérard, she had told them this would come to no good end, the unhealthy idleness, the laziness, now do you see what I mean? Even Doudouline's rock opera was disturbing, Baby Doc she could accept, but when it was a question of ten-year-old schoolchildren using drugs, no, that wasn't true, why write it into an opera, she would protest, and Polydor was putting away the dishes, there were scraps of pizza lying around on the living room table when Sophie appeared in her gray suit, she was even wearing a black scarf around her neck, thought Doudouline, as if her mother, like that scarf, had suddenly coveted a part of her pain; grief, misery belonged exclusively to the girls of the group, not to Sophie, and that other word must not yet be pronounced, that misery, that mourning, no, it must not be pronounced, after all, Gérard had never gotten the part in Sophie's Molière play, pain, grief, ought to remain with us. Sophie said, fixing her eyes on Doudouline's round chest, "Alright, enough crying, I know what we're going to do with Gérard, get your coats, girls, let's go, move." And Doudouline thought as she looked at her mother, Mother is playing a Euripides character, in her ugly suit, perched on her high heels to better give us orders, but in a spontaneous gesture that astonished Polydor, Sophie walked up to Doudouline who was still sitting in front of her pizza and wrapped her hands around her head, murmuring "Ah, my poor children, my poor children!" in a voice suddenly broken with emotion. This action seemed as protective as it did possessive, for Doudouline's blue eyes never should have cried, already their clarity was darkening in the bitter, vile substance of the first tears of mourning, that word, they would have to utter it soon. "It is a great mourning," said Sophie, running her long fingers through Doudouline's hair, her short hair that still sparkled with gold, wasn't she compassionate and clumsy like before, when she was pregnant, this repulsed her, for when she had pronounced the word "mourning," every one of the girls had given her a hard, ferocious look, she had felt those looks running up and down her back and thought clumsy, I'm clumsy, you have to say these things as they are, you have to say them. Swaying on her high heels, Sophie waited, listened, then began again in the same deferential voice, yes, this morning, it wasn't an ordinary ceremony but something sacred, death, cremation, oh, what's it called, help me Doudouline, but it was very short, said Doudouline, crying, Mother, it's called an incineration, because of the cognac, the sleeping pills, said Sophie, she didn't have time to suffer, thought Thérèse, and we'll soon go up the mountain, she said, leaning over to tie the laces of her sneakers, and Abeille brought her hand to her heart. It was a white day, a funereal day, and Thérèse — Abeille had once called her her Giantess in intimacy, she could double over so easily for herself, that tall, healthy stalk whose studious shadow was now an encumberment to her in her buildings, with her giant arms and feet, lacing up her sneakers with the soles toughened by walking — was going to go running on the mountain like before, wasn't one day for her just like any other? She would go towards the line of the sun that paled so quickly on the horizon in winter while, in Abeille's living room, the cracks were still there in the ceiling of her bedroom, in their distressing multiplicity, while Gérard was still there in the room, Gérard, who they didn't know what to do with. "The mountain," Thérèse had said, to leave her soul up there in the unbreathable air of our false peaks, air that burned on contact, for Gérard was still hot, burning intolerably, her bones, her heart afire, thought Abeille, and Paula was striding along the avenue, the cold wind blowing her hair out of its elastic so that it fell onto her hollow cheeks, holding her large portfolio of drawings in one hand that was clenched against the cold, and it seemed to her that her heart was beating too hard against her ribs, this pounding was unpleasant, as if Paula were walking inside a drum, she would quit smoking one day, but for now, a cigarette was still hanging from her lips; an attack, the doctor had said, you'll have an attack, at least she'd lived well, she thought — an attack! They didn't know anything about her, those adolescent doctors who were still wet behind the ears, who did they think they were to teach her morals? If her heart beat irregularly, it was because of that girl, Abeille, she thought, Paula had snapped at her quite a bit in her states of jealousy, but there was no cause to run away like the hare fleeing the hunter, and who had she left her for, all that was unclear, who wouldn't have gotten angry in the face of such stupidity, Abeille hadn't known how to appreciate her, Paula, her maturity, her depth, Paula belonged to a thinking generation, like Sophie, who had labored away at her Strindberg, like Cécile, Abeille's mother, with her discoveries of musical structures, and today her daughter listened to that Michael Jackson, a sort of decadent, Chopinesque romanticism had slowly deteriorated Abeille's mother, lamentable, lamentable, all of that was —

oh, that she not slip in dog shit like the last time, a month in a cast because of her wide, flat feet — and now Paula was giving evening courses to all those illiterates from the Beaux-Arts, from the university, for free, she was so disillusioned, she hadn't had Abeille's mother, too chaste for Paula, she could congratulate herself on having had the daughter, it was charming but bitter at that age, Cécile had been faithful to a military husband, a nice guy in the army who had understood nothing of her music, at the end she became delirious in the hospital. A privileged bond between her and Abeille, such heartbreak to see that at the end, and Paula heard her heart beating very hard against her ribs, it was true that she had been a bit violent, but in life one must forgive, Paula forgave well herself, she could see that they had never received the blows of a leather belt on their buttocks, moreover, how to get rid of your sisters, recipe for getting rid of your sisters one day when you're bored, and Paula mused with despair that today was the day Madame Boudreau came, and that when she went back to her cleaned, attentively waxed apartment during the night, she would see, when she turned on the light, those dust-covers on the living room chairs, and no silhouette absorbed in painting or drawing behind the stained glass door of the living room, she was sure to find herself someone for the night, otherwise she'd go to the Club, the exhausted gatherings that were there at dawn were often waiting for nothing but that. But Abeille was plump, mossy, you could hold onto her by the warmth between her legs, touching, attacking, the daughter or son of the doctor should have been a surgeon, a surgeon, and all this time, the etchings were drying out in the basement, and that picture of the black charred tree in that garden in Paris, if she had taken it out so many times it was to offer it to Abeille, make it a gift for her, that evening, Abeille who wouldn't be there when Paula came back late that night, a cigarette trembling on her lips, her sparse hair on her hollow cheeks.

You would have thought Gérard was still there, slumped in Abeille's velvet armchair, thought Johnie, they had once loved each other so much, in that beat-up furniture near the bridge, her long eyelashes that caressed your face, her cheeks of marble, her curly hair, and suddenly that vision of their legs as they rolled over each other lazily in the king-size bed they'd bought on credit, but get dressed, why are you all looking at me in that sanctimonious way, said Sophie, we're going out in my car now with Gérard, it's time now, we'll go to the bridge and stop above the river, Doudouline, where are the flowers, we'll need flowers too — and Thérèse was already running toward the mountain, up there, she'd feel better up there, in certain countries, when you passed through that unhealthy area above the hills, the mountains, far from the dirty smog of the cities, you suddenly came upon grandiose landscapes where herds of cows were grazing under a blue sky, the innocence of nature, her rural fairy, would there come a time when you would see them no more except in photographs on postcards? — and the armed Mountie was passing under the snowy branches on horseback, he was monstrously fat and nonchalantly ascending the mountain, his gloved hand sometimes reaching to touch his revolver, up there, she'll be happy up there. Why hadn't Thérèse flushed all those Valium at once down the toilet? And now it was too late, the blaze had been lit during the night, there was nothing left of Gérard, we'll stop on the river and pray, Sophie said, and

Doudouline roughly pushed her mother away and said "Please, Mother, be quiet!" "Your father didn't want you to be baptized, those intellectuals of the left, and we'll go by the river," Sophie persisted in a theatrical tone, "and there Gérard can fly away, she'll be liberated, the air will do her good, she'll take her leave along the river, the sea." "The Atlantic, she only liked the Atlantic," said Doudouline. "We went there to dance with girls in the evening, by the light of the moon, the bars were always full to the point of bursting. Those red lights in the streets, you remember, Abeille," said Doudouline, blowing her nose with a long blast. "It's awful what's happening to us, so awful, Gérard who didn't like the water, who never wanted to go swimming in a lake because the water was too cold." And the girls went out with their coats thrown over their shoulders, too preoccupied to put them on, forgetting the canvas on Abeille's easel and their cigarettes that were still smoking in the ashtrays, Gérard was there among them, still hot like a rain of fire in the metal box, thought Abeille, and Johnie, sitting next to Sophie who was driving the car was holding her on her lap, Doudouline, Abeille, Polydor were curled up against one another in the back, and her hands were trembling on the wheel. Sophie was thinking that she was guilty as a mother. Why hadn't she prevented a catastrophe like this? And Johnie's stoic profile next to her, Johnie who wasn't crying, wasn't that face accusing her? Guilty of not having offered Gérard a part in her Molière play, she could have, she was the director, but that unfortunate reticence she'd sensed, Gérard repeating to her that life was nothing, no, Sophie had said no, and the part had been refused her at the last minute. "Oh! Life is nothing," Gérard said laughing, and those parents who attended the memorial service without words or tears, looking lost, poor old people, but it was a very short ceremony, repeated Doudouline, again reprimanding her mother for driving too fast, there was no rush to get to the bridge, along the river, they could wander like that all night until they got to the sea, and in her grey suit with the black scarf knotted at her neck, Sophie thought again, I'm guilty, yes, that day with the silver, when Gérard had misplaced a silver fork in the drawer, didn't I scream? The silver, the books in the library, the crystal glasses, they misplaced everything, those girls, and soon it would be night on the lit-up bridge and river, thought Johnie, it was here, right nearby, in one of those slum buildings, one of those slum buildings that the flames would soon devour, that they had embraced and loved, Johnie, Gérard, in that bed they'd bought on credit, and the slow, lazy movements of Gérard's when she went to sleep next to her, exuding all around her enigmatic night, that collection of thin ribs and the crown of her black hair on the pillow. Sophie was saying now that perhaps it was time to stop, the river was calm beneath the snow, the snow that was melting already, and Doudouline bowed before the applause, on the stage where she had known exaltation, joy. The glorious bouquet of roses would soon be thrown into the river, the sea, the ocean where Gérard had danced with other girls on the docks, the beaches at night, near the Atlantic, the roses and Gérard under the muddy waters of the river when it was so cold, and what was the rallying cry the Spanish shepherds used among themselves, Lynda imitated it so well, when they got lost at night in their pastures, it wasn't a shout but a rough, wild sob that rose from Lynda's throat, the sheep fled into the hills when they heard that cry, it was a desperate but quivering roar, the vocal cords burned, throbbing, wailing, the cry of love like the cry of death, thought Johnie, it felt to her like that cry was rising to her lips, cold tears wet her cheeks. And Sophie put on the brakes, everyone got out of the car, it is a great mourning, said Sophie, let's go, girls, it's cold and we're shivering, good-bye Gérard, a minute of silence, please, and Doudouline threw her roses into the water, the wind and rain and snow, and soon it was Gérard's turn to be scattered into the wind, the rain and snow, Polydor saw a sculpture of Christ in a cathedral in Krakow, its body stretched forward like an arrow, the hands and feet coming off into loving flight, separating themselves from the nails in the cross, and she recited in a low voice in the twilight:

"Where have You hidden,
Beloved, and left me moaning?
You fled like the stag
After wounding me;
I went out calling You and You were gone."*

And it was night, almost dawn, Johnie, Polydor, Doudouline, Thérèse had gathered together again in Abeille's living room, twenty candles were burning themselves out on Gérard's birthday cake, Sophie would be there soon with the champagne, and Johnie thought about those who were marked with the Pink Triangle, thrown with the ashes and flowers, amid friends and parents, from a boat, a yacht, amid tears and suffering into San Francisco Bay which from then on would be the tomb of youth, in the waves, under a magnificent sun. They were all disappearing, children, young people, black or white, in a rain of fire and roses, and Johnie said "Till we meet again, Gérard, happy birthday, Gérard," and they all joined hands in a chain, repeating "Happy birthday, Gérard" as twenty candles burned themselves out on a birthday cake.

* Saint John of the Cross. *The Collected Works of Saint John of the Cross*. Trans. Kieran Kavanaugh, O.C.D., and Otilio Rodriguez, O.C.D. New York: Doubleday, 1964. 410.